TWO to

TWO to ONE

Poems & Short Stories

John Tissandier

First published 2019

Copyright © 2019 John Tissandier

ISBN: 978 1 795253 49 9

Cover image by John Tissandier

"Same reality, different dreams."

Foyen

Acknowledgements

Some of these poems and stories have been published in *Caduceus*, *International Times*, and *Self Enquiry*.

I would especially like to thank Alex Tissandier, John Elford, and Terry McDowell for helping me produce this book. I would also like to thank all the people who have organised poetry and creative writing groups in Totnes over the past ten years. Finally, I'm indebted to Jay Ramsay, who sadly passed away in December, for encouraging me to believe in myself as a poet.

The photo of the author is by Gemma Varney.

Contents

A WALK IN THE PEAK DISTRICT

Above me clouds embrace, effortlessly
Resolving the equations of the sky.
Sheep find rough grass sandwiched between rocks
And poets gorge themselves on butterflies.
The world is a scene painted on silence
By a painter who does not sign his name.
Even the breeze blowing over the dales'
Secret places cannot say what it is.
The beauty of the day flares briefly, but
Touched by the timeless this walk never ends.

BECAUSE I LIVE IN TOTNES

In my eye a transcendental gleam
In my bag the Transition Town Scheme
Because I live in Totnes

Just a few yards Arcturus nears
Not 36.7 light years
Because I live in Totnes

Greenlife, Riverford, Sacks and Seeds
Temples serving organic needs
Here in Totnes

Who needs supermarkets for protein?
Planting nut trees is the routine
Here in Totnes

Find yourself with psychotherapy
Lose yourself in nonduality
Just another day in Totnes

Weirdness, wholeness, incense, candles,
Goddesses in sandals,
Angels around us here in Totnes

Some say our manner is precious
I wonder are they jealous
Of the folk who live in Totnes?

Life's all change and transition
Except for the location
Our intention's to stay in Totnes

THE SECRET THERAPY

It doesn't matter
>   what essential oils you use
It doesn't matter
>   which stubborn knots you unloose
It doesn't matter
>   if it feels sharp or diffuse

It's your warm touch that heals

It doesn't matter
>   what shamanic tales you tell
It doesn't matter
>   how you incant magic spells
It doesn't matter
>   that you strike gongs, bowls and bells

It's your soft voice that heals

It doesn't matter
>   you trained as a therapist
It doesn't matter
>   you're a practising Buddhist
It doesn't matter
>   your crystals are the biggest

It's your beauty that heals

THE IMAGINARY STRUGGLE

I joined the circus of the gurus
      but I was not enlightened
I meditated for thirty years
      but I was not enlightened
I read the books of Eckhart Tolle
      but I was not enlightened
I heard the sound of one hand clapping
      but I was not enlightened
Then I experienced enlightenment...
      but I was not enlightened
Finally, I gave up searching for
      upgrades to reality
It was the end of thinking I was
      or was not
Enlightened

THE TREE OF KNOWLEDGE

When you accept a conclusion, or an answer,
it means you've settled on a particular branch.

But when you ask a question, it's like hovering
in the air before you choose a perch to sit on.

If you can find a question that has no answer,
it's like flying forever.

You become one with the sky.

THE ELUSIVE OBVIOUS

Vibrating birds on swaying branches
the warmth of passing cows
a thousand shades of green
the indecision of a fly.

Nameless, I name these things
all the while seeking the elusive
raspberry pip between my teeth.

NO MAN

I'm not looking out through two holes in my head
there is no separate little man here
the birds are speaking inside "me"
the Douglas-firs are waving inside "me"
everything mysteriously intimate

the One has many mouths
producing worlds out of emptiness
where a head should be

THE WRONG KIND OF WIND

He's a prisoner of science
incarcerated in a cramped habitat
sharing stale air with six strangers.
Fart jokes no longer seem funny and
he may yet crack under the pressure.

True, he sees glorious stars,
but they are outside – a place
he cannot touch.
He's a potted plant, cut off from its source,
just as plants are like astronauts
in their capsules of soil.

He joins in the micro-gravity tomfoolery
and the messages sent back to Earth are jovial,
but this quasi-Martian knows better than most
that our dreams of Mars are a distraction.
Although millions of miles from home
it's only now he sees what's on his doorstep:
his eyes filled with green, a fresh breeze on his face.

THE OUTLIER

Slipping
off the edge
into the Ocean
face golden
in the western setting sun
your gaze
fixed homewards.

In the end
what could I have done?
I was there
but merely scratched the surface of your depths
and yet...
your familiar pattern flows in my veins
a tributary of this vast Ocean
which has eroded the chalk
inside your mouth
so that now
you no longer speak to me.

Farewell
my friend
mother
father
without knowing it
I kissed your cheek
for the last time.

THERE'S A POET IN ALL OF US

There's a poet in all of us,
I confronted mine last night.
"You're living here rent-free," I cried,
"and sometimes you leave on the light."

I said to my inner poet,
"Times are tough, can't afford the waste."
"It would be a shame," he replied,
"if I disappeared without trace."

"You say that," I remonstrated,
"and you blab my innermost secrets."
"Yes, I know," he retorted, "but
that's your strength, not a weakness.

I speak the truth about your life.
Why is it that you would hide
the gateway to a secret place
that only the heart can find?"

"Fine words, fine words," I muttered,
"but often too repetitive.
You think you're some kind of seismograph,
but you're just a bit too sensitive."

"Well," he admitted, "takes courage
to expose the poet inside.
Be brave and show your soul, open
the curtains and let in the light!

If I stay I'll write more poems,
self-publish them and be damned.
It will be *your* name on the cover
so then you'll realise who I am!"

THE DAY I ESCAPED MY TIGHT UNDERWEAR

"Women's underwear holds things up
Men's underwear holds things down"
Who can forget these immortal lines
from *Underwear* by Ferlinghetti?
The first poem I ever liked
passed on by a friend
and not read in a Lit class.
Later I challenged my teacher
Why? Why did you hide this
amazing arrhythmic unpunctuated stuff?
He said it's a matter of order
you have to start with the classics
work your way down
Blake
Browning
Betjeman...
till one day you become ready
for Ginsberg and Ferlinghetti
(Of course he didn't say that exactly
he'd never even heard of the Beat poets)
but who wants to see regulation knickers
when you can admire a sexy thong?
I said you're wrong!
He remained rigid in his views
maybe he wore a fascist girdle...
At eighteen I exposed myself
I came out and announced
I loved poetry
and you're right Lawrence – poetry
is the underwear of the soul.

THE PARROT AND THE NIGHTINGALE

bright beady eye and squawky voice
telling me words I already know
copies of my very own thoughts

the nightingale sings otherworldly notes
yet I recognise the beauty that
flies up from deep within my soul

THE BUDDHAS AND THE BEES

Lips puckered, cheeks hollow,
devotees sip the nectar of wisdom
through tiny conceptual straws,
while prostrating before lifeless Buddhas.

Hairy honey bees alight
on sublimely coloured beepads
and leave heavenwards,
proboscises dripping with bliss.

THE WISE IDIOT

everything is all there is
so I talk about it
everything on my plate

a tomato is all there is
so I talk about it
a tomato on my plate

nothing is all there is
so I talk about it
nothing on my plate

THE BEACH HUTS

42 sky blue
43 colour of sea
44 maroon door
45 nowhere to be seen
46 sunburned pink
47 blue heaven
48 purple mistake
49 orangey shine
50 red mystery

out at sea billowing sails
white light racing across the bay

MIRROR, MIRROR ON THE WORLD

The hand that holds the pen
that writes this poem
looks unfamiliar;
the eyes that see the words
being written blink in surprise.
The mind – this human mind – is
ready to sign its name,
but from where the words are coming from
in truth it cannot say.

When I was a child
sometimes I would convince myself
that the figure in the mirror was real,
and when I held two mirrors
an infinity of selves was revealed,
one fairer and wiser than me.
I make sense by reflecting his mirror-writing.

SUNDAY CHAT

(to my mother 1924-2016)

I'm still getting used to being everywhere
rather than located in one place, though
when you call I'm always sitting in my
usual spot overlooking the canal.
It was seeing a beautiful swan that
made me buy this flat, but no swans today.
For lunch I'm going to eat a steak I had
with your father in 1943.
And the rest of the day? Why sleep of course!
That's all I do now except for our chats;
I'm glad they give you a chance to practise
your mother tongue and to hear your original name.
A mother's work is never done of course:
I have my role, which is to guide your thoughts,
but after a long lifetime of practice
it's become completely effortless now.
Last Sunday I had some wine – just a glass –
but with my wrist I didn't pour well;
red drops slid slowly down the bottle...
I watched for what felt an eternity.

RATATOUILLE NICOISE

You lie there on my plate,
steaming lightly... a stew certainly,
but one with a certain *je ne sais quoi.*
You're next to the Japanese tempeh and,
without waving a *tricolore*, evoke
memories of my father down south.
He's returning smiling from the local
market with his practical string bag,
stuffed royally with mediterranean sunshine.

TONTON LUCIEN

Tonton Lucien sits on the bank
of the pea-green Marne,
fishing rod held hopefully.
Claude and I, on the passerelle,
whisper and throw a pebble in.
"Oh, regardez la belle!" he cries.
We scamper back to join him
and chuckle as he tells us
of the fish he thinks he's seen.

In his shabby suit and 'tache,
with gesticulating cane,
he could be Charlie Chaplin.
He stops in the street abruptly:
"Once upon a time," he tells us,
"nobody owned anything,
then this petit bonhomme comes along
with miles of fencing
and now everything is his!"

In the café by the carrefour
he orders un verre de rouge
and tall glasses of grenadine.
We drink in the icy red colour,
laughing as he tells us jokes
about our father.
Nose sharp and inquisitive, a
laugh that's hoarse and throaty,
his eyes twinkle mischievously.

Sundays he doesn't go to church;
if he prays at all it's to
the gods Darwin, Einstein and Freud.
He makes precision instruments for scientists,
deep in the bowels of the Sorbonne.

Tonton Lucien can fix things
and improvising with bent pins
makes dead machines sing again.
Once he came to England
and performed his Lazarus trick
on a-car-that-wouldn't-go.
Fellow mechanics were épatés
and ordered drinks for the hero!

At seventeen, his legs lagged
with newspaper, he mended vehicles
in freezing Parisian workshops.
Then sent to Germany,
he worked in the labour camps
(appendix removed without anaesthesia).
But *I* see him savouring
a Bourgogne, or bone-dry Sancerre,
as happy as a sand-boy.

Tonton Lucien's favourite story
was about faking his own death,
drill a hole in his coffin
to see who turns up at the end.
If there was a way to pierce
the veil that separates us
he would have found it by now.
So it's goodbye Tonton Lucien –
no celestial vineyard for you!

And yet, I hear him sing:
"A Joinville le Pont pon pon, Chez Gégène, Chez Gégène..."

PARC BENCH rev.1

Children play
people stroll by
but they might as well not be there

He keeps thinking he hears "ping ping"
but it's only the play of imagination
and the birds singing

Nobody knows what he's had for breakfast
or what he's listening to
he continues to make observations on life
but "life" is no longer interested in him

Once he was connected to thousands
a bright star in a constellation of data
now he's a dead rock
adrift in deep space
no-one can reach him

His agitated fingers move uselessly
like the legs of an upturned beetle
longing for the feel of plastic

He's haemorrhaging reality
desperately in need of a data transfusion
an email, a Facebook comment, anything
to confirm he lives
he needs bits to make IT

Colours are washed out by the harsh midday sun
oh for the cool softness of a liquid crystal display
yesterday he was an archipelago
today a lost island off the shipping lanes
he's going crazy with the need to trade trivia
and he fears by the time he's back online
cyberspace will have become unfamiliar

Someone sits on the bench next to him
a dormant sense awakens
strong perfume
unrecognised undertones...
Do I smell too? he wonders
What are the communication protocols of smell?
Is there a TCP/IP for the olfactory network?
He feels the breeze on his skin
a carrier wave for aromatic data
modulated by flowers, grass, trees

Sniffing like a hound
he begins to wonder
What other senses have I mislaid?
What other dimensions?

REAL NERDS DON'T NEED COMPUTERS

He lies on his Tintin towel, facing the hairy sand dunes,
attention not on the epic sandcastling and wild splashing;
he doesn't seem to feel the noonday sun dropping photons
as weighty as melons onto the pink target of his back,
or hear the cries of "chouchou" and "chi-chi"
from the beach sellers.
Using only pencil and paper he's writing a program,
a solitary surfer on wave after wave of Fortran.

Now he lifts his head momentarily,
a naked tanned woman is approaching;
she saunters lazily down to the sea,
toes squeezing and releasing the hot sand.
Two eyes, two arms, two legs, two loud nipples;
creation is binary and that's good.

While families pack their parasols
he checks his program carefully,
using the wetware of his brain
as the processor.

***

Back home
the kettle and
computer switched on,
his paper-based thoughts
keyed-in, becoming
64-bit streams
of zeros and ones.
Excitement rising
he presses a key –
it actually works!
Feelings of relief
initiated,
big smile uploaded.

Brilliant holiday!

GARDEN

sometimes
I go out
and pretend to be me
but all the while
I remain
in a garden of green
many shades
one colour
and who can stop the wind
it blows where it will
moving everything
yet at the garden's centre
all remains
perfectly still

THE A-LIST FLY

The little fly lives in a palace,
looked after by a team of fifty.
Its health is carefully monitored;
its erratic flight pattern studied.
The little fly is king ever since
other species became extinct.

JACQUARD'S DREAM

(to Joseph Marie Jacquard)

hole
not a hole
hole
not a hole
hole hole
not a hole
hole not a hole not a hole
from such simple beginnings
is woven a complex reality
I walk on a carpet of atoms
through a shimmering tapestry of light

0
1
0
1
0 0
1
0 1 1
Facebook Twitter Email Text
weaving encounters across
the fabric of hyperspace
dark cables lit up by laughter
continents connected by multiplexed love & hate

there is a tapestry
I am woven into it
as is everyone I have ever known
and every place I've ever been
and every thought I've ever schemed

frozen in the tapestry
is a trapped figure
tearing frantically at the edge
looking for a thread
as if to pull with superhuman strength
and make the universe unravel

vibration
void
vibration
void
vibration
void...

word

word

word
not a word

CRISIS IN EXCELSIS

Who believes there is a God:
the bankers who loaned thousands
or the recipient without a job?
The bankers who brought down the economy
or the man who lost his home?

Yes, who believes there is a God:
the fraudulent bankers who got away scot-free
or the angry people who were wronged?

    3 World Wars
    49 Moon landings
    386 years without poverty
    that's how much it cost the taxpayers
    to bailout Wall Street banking.

In their rare moment of weakness
the dragons should have been dismembered.
But it's business as usual:
Regulation-lite markets
dominated by the few;
money buying power,
power generating money;
midnight threats to presidents,
democracies brought down
by the snap of a finger.

Who believes in *bankers*?
Well not Jesus
who cleansed the temple of greed.

Bankers are not clever
but they employed ex-rocket scientists
who magicked formulas
to generate wealth without risk;
they took it on trust
none of the bankers grasped the details.
Why didn't they intuit
that laws governing space
cannot predict the future reliably
when it's filled with people?

Who believes there is a God:
The bankers orchestrating brainwashing
or young people imprisoned for debt?
The bankers looting a planet
or the rioters trashing a store?

Yes, who says, "We got away with it.
Alleluia, it's a miracle!"
It's the bankers
whose private helicopter
hovers above
like the angel of death
while below them
the world is consumed.

ABOUT THE SIZE OF IT

She stares at the rolling waves
then dips an empty Thermos cup
into the sea and lets the water fall;
as many atoms there as cups of water
in all the oceans of the world.

How can anything so minuscule
result in something so momentous?
On her cheek a single tear
hinting at a million things I never did.

The sky crr crrrrr cries
a crazy cyclotron of seagulls,
the sand sucks and gasps
greedy for more and more;
every pebble is clearly seen
every clinging seaweed strand.

The atoms in her body squashed
with all the space removed
would be the size of a grain of sand,
yet too heavy to hold
in the palm of my hand.

I watch her escape,
everything I was anchored to
is vanishing,
whilst on the bloodshot horizon
a monstrous tsunami is gathering...

LUCKY CAT

a multitude of ghosts
inhabiting a quantum world
bang on the walls of virtuality
but they cannot be heard here
where the birds are singing

yes, I've been lucky
the wave function of the universe
collapsed into me
I'M HERE where the air is sticky
as real as a potentially unreal being can be

COUNTDOWN

10	Noah must have had a mighty big ship
9	to hold two of every animal
8	so many species to pack in
7	only gopher wood and pitch
6	but a future Noah
5	would find it easy
4	with CAD and steel
3	the cargo
2	only
1	Man

THE WHOLE OF HIS LIFE

During the day
he kept the garden alive
with a small watering can.
When evening came
he lost himself in the quiet sounds
of a xylophone.
He smiled occasionally, but spoke
to no one.

An acute observer
examining his dead body
wouldn't suspect
the whole of his life he
never once
used the front door.

MADRID MERMAID

(to Ruth)

I feel like a stranded mermaid
a fish without a home
had to escape the tentacles
that strangled me with love

I hardly had a peseta
just a case full of chords
I walked the lonely boulevards
listening to Thom Yorke

but I planted a little seed
and watched it grow each day
sheltered it with cool music
from the heat and the rain

now my life is easier
but when I close my eyes
the briny wind calls me
to swim beneath the sky

RING OF TREES

Is this the ring of trees
where Hermes appeared?

There are signs of cattle having rested here.
A rope swings in the breeze
and there's a glint of river through the leaves,
but no god comes to seek me out:
no golden staff, no winged sandals, no flute or lyre.

I perch on a deviant trunk
bent at ninety degrees,
the tree created a convenient seat
and then
remembered the way up.

So easy to believe magic could happen
enclosed by this circle,
no gossiping birds,
no nibbling squirrels,
this is a place reserved for dreams.

I stay
rooted to the spot
descending ever deeper...
but my twitchy human legs
are not ready to walk through endless shadows.
Leaving without seeing the god of writing
I slither down the grassy slope
to a tree-lined path, entwined with words,
that takes me home.

SUNDAY MORNING

A blind man whistles a tune,
a dog walker follows her dog,
church bells exercise their right
to minify sleep.
The sun is obscured by clouds,
but there's enough light to see
that the sun is obscured by clouds.
Intriguing patterns appear on
the surface of puddles by
the River Dart.
The blind man returns – now
he's singing – his
vision unobscured.

LUNCH

My beetroot-red mouth
kisses white bread, not
something the queen would do.
The wine tall on the table,
one state closer to transcendence,
its molecules free to swirl
unlike the food it surveys.
The avocados so perfect
I almost cry. When
will I see their likes again?
The tiny blue light on my phone
flashes persistently, but in vain.
Ripping the bread in two I notice
that one piece looks like a mouth;
yes, all over the world mouths
are being eaten by bigger mouths,
and stars are being sucked up by black holes
like so much spaghetti.
I read while I eat,
digesting words that taste
like they've been dipped in a piquant sauce.
Some say it's all a dream, but the celery
and carrot sticks deny it,
making loud ontological statements
about the crunchiness of reality.
Now the plate is empty, my mouth still;
in a few hours a transformed tomato will stare out of my eyes
and begin to type these wOrds.
It thinks: "What am I? Where do I come from?
Where am I going?" But let's not go there.
There is one small piece of bread remaining,
full of h o l e s,
peering through a hole I see the whole universe.

BRIGHTON BEACH AND OTHER FORMS OF MADNESS

On Brighton beach
with my notebook, watching
the lazy grey sea and
strolling gay couples
gorgeous as tropical fish.
A tap on the shoulder
"Are you writing a poem?"
Startled I nod, he laughs
"I bet my mate you were a poet!"
He snatches my notebook
"A gem! A little universe,
with its own rules.
My name is David Smith, by the way,
I'm a literary agent."
We exchange emails;
I send poems, he sends praise.
He calls me a visionary,
a 21st century Blake,
he says I see things, I see things
others cannot see.

He finds a publisher;
excited, I await an advance.
Then nothing...
October comes
and aerial migrants from Scandinavia
with thrilling displays of
organized randomness.

I track him down,
a surly individual opens the door –
his brother – but he won't talk.
With the help of several pints

the story is flushed out:
the day they had to call for help;
how he told them his name
was David Christ Smith.
I write down directions to the hospital
in my notebook.
An agent? Yes, David
is a door-to-door sales agent.
But he sees things, he sees things
others cannot see. The
rules of his universe are
peculiar to him.

Mocked by seagulls
I follow the shoreline back home,
past the ruined dreams of the West Pier,
past the crap of ice-cream wrappers.
On a sudden impulse
I throw my notebook into the icy Channel
and for a brief moment
my imagination is still.

SO WHAT'S THE DIFFERENCE?

So what's the difference between sitting down there and standing
up here?

Down there
> it's plain vanilla actuality
Up here
> it's an augmented reality

Down there
> I don't have to spill the beans
Up here
> everyone gets to know my dreams

Down there
> I'm just an unknown scrawler
Up here
> I save a quid and get to be taller

Down there
> you can't see if my flies are undone
Up here
> it's obvious to everyone

Down there
> It's like relaxing sightseeing
Up here
> I'm the focus for the time being

Down there
> No-one gives a shit about my views
Up here
> Some are wondering, "Who the fuck are you?"

Down there
      I talk like the rest of the crowd
Up here
      "I wandered lonely as a cloud..."

Down there
      my stupidities are confined
Up here
      I put my ass on the line

Down there
      I can be as quiet as a little mouse
Up here
      I'm the opposite of anonymous

Down there
      Who I am is not apparent
Up here
      Suddenly I become transparent

Down there
      I'm just so-and-so
Up here
      I can be famous like Jackie Juno

Down there
      I don't risk a banana peel
Up here
      I share things and make them feel real

Down there
      is beckoning, it's the end of being
Up here
      by my reckoning. Enjoy your evening!

ARE YOU LISTENING?

Are you listening?
Or have you drifted off already
thinking
"What shall I eat later?"

Do I have your attention?
There will be a test!

Are you listening to me
or to the sounds around?
[Insert as appropriate, e.g. people talking outside, the hum of a
fan, etc.]

Is this poem even written down
or
am I making it up
as I go along?

Well having started
let's carry on
with an occasional "**SHOUT**"
to bring back the drifters.
I once saw a woman leap out of her seat at a concert
when the drums and cymbals
played a loud crescendo;
that was the composer getting his own back:
"Madam, how dare you sleep during my concerto!"

***

Oh
but I know
it's so hard to listen.
Why listen to me
when YOU are the most fascinating thing
in this whole universe?
Right now your thoughts are dancing by
like a Brazilian carnival,
or in the case of [Insert the name of a pompous person present]
a procession of holy relics.

But maybe you're thinking:
"Write something beautiful,
say something moving,
something I've never heard before –
then I'll listen.
I don't want your pushy poetry
doing in my distractions."

Ah yes,
but to write something beautiful
requires a poet,
whereas maybe
all I'm doing
is stringing words together
for as long as I can
until the jig is up
and I'm found out...

***

Ladies and gentleman,
this is your poet speaking.
Please remain seated in case
of turbulent rhythms and poor rhymes.
If you look below
you'll see we're cruising above [Insert a description of the floor,
e.g. a worn flowery carpet, etc.]
With the tailwind on our side
we shall be ending shortly.
The weather in [Insert location] is [Insert weather description, e.g.
cloudy with a temperature of 7 degrees centigrade, etc.]
On behalf of all the words in this poem
and the rest of the crew,
I'd like to thank you folks for listening to us today.
We hope you had a pleasant voyage
free of Andrew Motion sickness.
Please do not attempt to leave this poem until
my voice has stopped completely.
As you exit the poem make sure you gather all your thoughts
and have your applause ready for inspection.
Thank you for your patience,
we are now cleared for ending.

COLOUR CATASTROPHE

Gran, Gran, why are you smiling?
Everyone's miserable,
but you look so happy.
My dear, my wide-eyed child:
Winston's coat is black and white, my
dog looks the same in this new light!

Gran, Gran, why aren't you negative?
All the colours have vanished,
the world has lost its shine.
My dear, grey-eyed ghostly one:
my shoes and skirt are black,
my hair and blouse are white
– in the mirror I look just right!

Gran, Gran, why so positive?
No more Dulux colour range,
the rainbow's looking very strange.
My dear, my disappointed one:
it's just a form of rationing;
we managed without oranges.
In a darkened living room,
I saw the queen land on the moon;
colourless flags brightly glowed
amongst the flickering shadows.

JOHN THE BAPTIST

the bell rings
I leap up
then I remember
I don't have a bell
unless...
a bell has been placed inside my home
put there when I wasn't looking
I become anxious
supposing my dog becomes conditioned
it's been known to happen
then I remember
I don't have a dog
unless...
a dog has been placed inside my home
put there when I wasn't looking
there's another sound
it isn't a bell
it isn't a dog
it's my knife and fork
clattering to the floor

THE WORLD

The Advaitin world
    like yours
        but with added awareness
The Buddhist world
    like yours
        but with added emptiness
The Catholic world
    like yours
        but with added guilt
The Quaker world
    like yours
        but with added silence

(Punctuated by sardines gurgling
    and seagulls eating chips)

John's world
    like yours
        but with added guitar solos
And this world
    like you
        exactly like you

Salty waves
    move across your eyeballs
and already you know
    what everything
        will taste of

THE GREAT DOUBT

An I-assuming fragment
carried far away from home on
the baroque palanquin of time.
One day the journey ends and I
find myself back where I started.
I've heard I'm supposed to be pleased,
but if home is so wonderful
then why did I ever leave?

SURFACES

The surface of my experience looks like a
room, but I don't know what is sustaining it:
a God, a brain or a microprocessor.
I've only just woken up here, but this room's
arranged as if someone's lived in it for years;
there's mementoes and piles of old newspapers.
I have a fantasy there's a plug somewhere
and if I pull it, everything will drain out.
Pinching myself is pointless: how can one tell
if the pain is real or imaginary?
Accompanied by a constant hum I walk
towards the sofa, where there's a strange blinking
that's like the vertical line of a cursor:
on off, on off, on off. Now it's on the wall,
now it's traversing what's called a window,
now it's changing the texture of the ceiling.
I am not what I think I am, the light is
fading, and soon all that remains of me will
have transmigrated to this printed surface.

NDE

Ah breathing
used to be so easy
didn't have to think about it
in out in out
just kept happening

But then I seemed to lose
the knack and
my lungs felt like they were stuffed
with old tissue

And it wasn't just the breathing
time stopped ticking

What happened next will sound like a cliché
I was propelled down a tunnel at great speed
towards a bright light obviously
but I was wrong
the light at the end of my tunnel was pitch black
I took this as a worrying sign...
I floundered about and found what felt like a giant light switch

I flicked the switch and was lit up
by the Light of all lights
it was so dazzling I couldn't see a bloody thing
and I knew there was nothing here
but this bright Light
for eternity

I wasn't ready
I belonged to the realm of shadows
so I flicked the giant switch to off and
found myself sitting
in the front row of a cinema
it was dark
and because it was dark I could see

The image on the screen
showed a child looking down at my popcorn with envy
as if it were real

THRUSTING INTO THE GREAT MYSTERY

Shiva laughs
as his phallus rises
to infinity.
Shakti presses him
to another climax and
is never tired of creating worlds
numberless as seeds.
Apparently two,
when their eyes meet their gaze
is one ocean of rapture.
Huge waves appear to move
across its surface,
but all remains still.

REINCARNATION

In ran Creation
suggesting that rather than Death as
an incinerator
reincarnation would make
a nice narration
but Being said au
contraire, inane
my friend – there is no
inner actor in a
unity!

SUNSET SOLILOQUY

When does a sunset start?
When the sun no longer fries your eyeballs I guess
and you see a streaky freaky psychedelic painting lacy in the sky
with dyed islands of red.

If you wish to write about a sunset for your poetry class
there'll probably be days of thick cloud,
but if you miss one somebody will approach you and say,
"Did you see the sunset last night? It was absolutely stunning. It
took my breath away."
No point asking for details; it's all second-hand.

Once I met a small boy and discovered he had a dog called Sam.
So I asked him, "What is Sam like?"
His little face scrunched up in concentration and he thought about
it a long time.
Finally he replied, "He's like Sam."
I declare, like the boy, that a sunset is like the unique sunset it is.

So if you want to know about sunsets don't listen to what I have
to say.
Whatever colours I spray on my poem (myriad shades of red,
yellow, orange, purple and pink),
or adjectives I employ (fiery, flaming, stunning, blushing), or how
far my lines stretch to emulate the horizon,
it's not the real sky.
The poet's magical powers mediated through language are limited:
the word "**FIERY**" writ large does not make the paper catch fire.

No poet has ever truly captured the climax of a beautiful sunset, because the only other thing that existed at that moment (apart from the sunset) was wordless amazement.
Poets can only write when they and words come back, but then sensation has faded,
and what they wished to write about has set behind the shadowy horizon of time.

A TRUE HEART

Can energy be extinguished?
Can the absolute vanish?

Thought cannot fill an infinite chasm.
A cudgel leaves no mark on the sky.

How to express the ineffable?
How to avoid the next fall?

Nobody can be 100 percent wrong.
No truism is 100 percent right.

Does a buzz fly or a fly buzz?
Do we need to be told that we are?

Your feet cannot walk away without you.
Your thoughts are not under your control.

Can faith be drowned by doubts?
Can a true heart ever be alone?

FIVE

(To Goldilocks)

I am just a five,
found at the mid-point
of a graph or knob;
on the left is less,
on the right much more.

I am a safe house
for those who don't know,
sit on the fence, or
hold fast when you ask:
whose side are you on?

Nought one two three four
six sept eight nine ten
would lead to war, you
need five to act as
a UN peace zone.

Not too thin or fat
not too hot or cold
not too bright or daft
not too shy or bold;
the wise know my worth.

Some might say I'm dull,
grey and Lib Dem; but
if your aim is to
rest at the still point,
then I'm your right hand.

DIVING IN

(to William Trubridge)

He lies on his yoga mat
eyes closed, stretches his body;
breathes in for five – out for ten.

He tries to empty his mind,
to find the space between thoughts –
no oxygen for thinking.

Now he's no longer on Earth,
but in zero gravity;
no stimuli distracts him
here in this silent abyss.
He's calm though he cannot breathe.

When it's time to return home,
the journey is exactly
one hundred and twelve metres.
First to appear, a wet hand
above the ocean's surface,
glistening in the sunlight as
if holding gold.

MEMORABLE 45s OF '62

the first record I ever bought
was Wonderful Land by the Shadows
I thought Hank Marvin looked cool
behind his specs and red Stratocaster

the second record I bought was Telstar
a hymn to the dawn of the new age
as my record revolved on its deck
so did Telstar spin through space
years later I was rudely brought down to Earth
by the discovery it was Maggie Thatcher's favourite

ENGLAND

There are no earthquakes here
This is a civilised country
Stiff upper lip and all that
We keep our tremors under control
My pent-up lust and volcanic rage
Are never going to blow
I'd rather shoot myself in the head!

OLD COUPLE

No dear, I didn't kiss you *twice* because I forgot;

I kissed you twice because I love you.

SHOPPING

enjoying warm affection
in the frozen food section
later our ice-creams start melting
on the checkout conveyor belt
I pay for my things and you
pay for your things, but back home
my things end up in your mouth
and your things end up in mine

SINCE WE PARTED

Since we parted
I eat the shadow of a strawberry
I see the wrong side of the dawn
I walk but not to your apartment
Another evening yawns

No, that's not it!
Since we parted
I eat *twice* as many strawberries
All the duvet is mine
I walk, but not through minefields, and
there's more in my bottle of wine

No, that's not it!
Since we parted
I cook but miss your compliments
I sleep and some nights I don't
I walk past memories of you

MY LAST DESIRE

Please try to forgive me,
this is
my last desire.
I've transcended everything
except
my last desire.
Some may judge me,
but try to understand
this is
my last desire.
I don't want to come back
to live another life.
Satchitananda is calling,
and what's dragging me back
is my last desire.
Can you not see
in order to be free
I have to rid myself
of my last desire?
I tried to satisfy it;
it gave God a good laugh.
So I nailed it to the ground,
but it just came bouncing back.
Then I tried meditation,
chanting, incense sticks,
standing on my head.
The great Ramana
shrugged and said, "You're on
your own here, Johnny T.
with the fire of
your last desire."

Some will say I'm a fool,
I should have transcended it;
failing that cut it off
with a carving knife,
or dialled 999.
All I can say is:
friends,
don't forsake me;
and do remember
this is
my last desire.
If it turns out to be
fool's gold then I'll know;
if it proves divine
then I think I'll be glad
I made it just in time
before dissolving
into the night.

THE SECRET OF LIFE

Falling from the cliff top

I enjoy the view

PRESENCE

soft belly
unclenched mind
radical
clarity
needs few words

REASONS TO BE CHEERFUL

Fresh flowers
April showers
awakening powers
more daylight hours

Lively discussions
chess with Russians
noisy percussion
without repercussion

Home-made cake
the Hippy Hippy shake
non-poisonous snakes
a bit of give and take

Sweet stores to explore
nothing to be sorry for
solos by Gilmour
stepping ashore

Table and chair oaken
not rude but outspoken
a child that's not woken
and silence unbroken

Seeing the Milky Way
being dad on father's day
Millet, Monet
and the Musée d'Orsay

Yes, these are reasons TO BE CHEERFUL

Dark red Bordeaux
the arrival of Godot
names like Limpopo
ha-ha-ha ho-ho-ho!

23 degree tilt
a world without guilt
living life to the hilt
'neath a patchwork quilt

A God with no beard
an effort that's cheered
a man who was jeered
now suddenly revered

Laces that don't snap
paths free of dog crap
a favourable trade gap
finding a dust cap

Sherlock Holmes
geodesic domes
a place to call home
the absence of gnomes

A perfect blend
bucking the trend
a very good friend
who knows when to end

are reasons TO BE CHEERFUL

WILD

Could I put together
some words that are so hot
the paper catches
fire?

Could I write something so
deep a pit appears in
the middle of the page
and the reader falls
in?

Could I write something so
beautiful and sexy
everyone falls wildly
in love with me?

Probably not

But the poet in me keeps
hopingwritingtrying.

A POEM ABOUT DUST

You fucking little piece of dust,
all you had to do was be
a piece of dust – that's all.
Some are called to be giant nebulae
and others brain surgeons;
all you had to be
was a tiny piece of dust.
Couldn't you manage that?
Lurk there quietly in a corner until noticed
and then climb aboard the pan when swept by the brush,
not escape underneath the lip like a frantic bug,
or dance around like a bleeding *prima donna*!
You annoying elusive fucking little piece of dust;
as if I didn't have enough to cope with!

DID I TELL YOU WE DRANK RUM?

Today the bin-men are playing kettledrums
accompanied by cranial thrumming,
pink elephants (or possibly car-horns)
provide occasional trumpeting.

An uncrumpling of complaining limbs
allows me to stand
facing the crumbliness of reality,
full spectrum nausea,
and in the mirror the simulacrum
of a human being.

Did we have sex?
Pain tells me it was more like a scrummage,
but she was scrumptious, strumpeting her stuff
while the band played rumba.
By the time we landed in the street
after a rumpus with a candelabrum
we'd drained the bottle.

Sounds emerge from the bathroom
and I'm scared
of the humdrumness revealed by daylight,
darkness is needed for dreams to last.
Swaying, wishing I was quadrumanous,
I recite my favourite mantram
to coordinate my
brumous thrummy cerebrum
Om Mani Padme Rum
trying to find the still centre
it proves to be no nostrum.

The door opens but there is no time
for good-mornings or decorum,
like a rocket-propelled panjandrum
I lurch towards the bowl,
exploding spectacularly
in rumbustical showers of frumenty
and rumbledethumps.
She stands by the door open-mouthed...
I cannot describe how I feel
lying rumdrunk on the bathroom floor
beyond the reach of dictionaries.

RAINSTICK

Waving cloudy flags
an army of giants
as wide as the horizon
drums on the rooves with sticks
and catapults dogs
that smack against the glass.

Arrows of lightning
strike the ground and
thunder rolls across the sky
like a trillion tins
tumbling down the Grand Canyon.

Fragments of heaven
whirl weirdly like witches
dispensing chaos
the weather ecstatic
the moon blown away
by the giants' trumpet blasts!

SATSNAG (sic)

before the satsang we enjoyed smoking
cups of Lapsang Souchong
and then the teacher began...
but the snag was I'd heard the metaphors before
the satsang felt stagnant

there were birds outside
they outsang the satsang
so I left for the garden

after a few Ashtanga asanas
I sucked a succulent satsuma

reality trickled down my chin
and I realised this singular moment
was worth more
than all the satangs in Thailand

NAKED

playing tennis
in a nudist colony
side by side
in a makeshift mortuary
dead
alive
having fun
naked

the butcher naked
the banker naked
the Virgin Mary naked and sacred

smooth spotty hairy wrinkly
honestly naked
beautifully naked
we meet at last without pretence
naked

APROPOS

(to Susan)

Apropos
       your trip to the Limpopo
              if you catch a tiger by the toe
                     let it go
              I don't know
       why you go
              to the Limpopo
                     but your nature is to to and fro
       go with the flow
              let your dreams grow
       so row row your boat across the Limpopo
              and have a laugh ho ho
                     on the banks of the Limpopo
                            there's buffalo and rhino
                                   a picture show
                     yes there's plenty of *eau* in the Limpopo
                            but don't drink it – oh, no, no!

ADOPTION

(to Ed)

He thought he heard a hen clucking;
it was gas in his intestines.
He failed to convince us that cruelty to poultry is predestined.

Battery hens don't know heaven, they've
never seen sun or breathed fresh air.
Abused, featherless, frustrated, they know only lives of despair.

Yet maybe there's a way out...
to adopt an ex-battery hen
and show it kindness in return for all those chicken breasts, Amen.

YEAH I WAS CRAZY

yeah I was crazy
to believe you can have a sunrise
without a sunset
my tortured mind craves an explanation
but this arid desert
provides not a drop of sense
crazy with love
I never saw it coming
this dreadful drought

EARLY 1 MORNING

not 1
not 2
but 3 pieces of toast
on my plate

the mind looking for meaning
and it's not yet 7

outside a white seagull
on a neighbour's roof
has 0 plans for the day

I write on the back cover
of my tiny noteb00k
because
all the pages are fu11

$$E = mc^2$$

E-volution is simply
increasing complexity
so that eventually
a brain is produced
that can see actually
it's all just Energy.

WINTER

the
tree
looks
out
at
whiteness

out
through
winter
at
the
whiteness
of
time

crystals
breaking
branches
like
the
falling
snow

WHO KILLED SOCIETY?

Their policies are extremely predatory
And manifesto fit for the lavatory
Their promises are brittle and transitory
What they say and what they do contradictory.

Increased poverty comes with the territory
Inequality practically mandatory
Up north the closure of another factory
Extra peers fit only for the crematory.

Yes I know what I said is derogatory
It's an inventory of why I don't vote Tory
For the details you'll have to study history
and George Osborne's excretory oratory.

Maggie's heart was kept in a refrigeratory
For the coalminers her reign terminatory
Her style was intimating and hectory
Nothing ever stood in the way of victory.

She and buddy Ronnie spun a little story
That it's best to be antiregulatory
they then dismantled all that was statutory
the banks were sent on a deadly trajectory.

So there you have it the unabridged backstory
To why you'll never persuade me to vote Tory
And the answer to the question is: Maggie
With a dagger in the conservatory.

A SIGHT TO DELIGHT IN?

I was a geographer
travelled the world
H U G E world
Now I'm old
SpaceHasShrunk

Lines of latitude and l
o
n
g
i
t
u
d
e

are tight round my throat

Features?
The only feature I see
is the waterfall rushing d
o
w
n
the lavatory bowl

ONCE I WAS X

I am a BASIC programmer but not now
I am a Logo programmer but not now
I am a Forth programmer but not now
I am a Pascal programmer but not now
I am a C programmer but not now
I am a 6502 programmer but not now
I am an 80x86 programmer but not now
I am a Lisp programmer but not now
I am a Visual Basic programmer but not now
I am a Python programmer but not now
I am a Delphi programmer but not now
I am a Java programmer but not now
I am a seeker but not now

SHORT UNTITLED POEMS

Just for a moment
Like a full stop in the sky
The moon stops the mind

Oh it's such a crime
All the flowers are hiding
Inside the darkness

"We know you're in there
Come out with your stamens up!"
Call the spring police

All the leaves are brown
Next year trees will be needing
Fresh solar panels

Central heating on
Helicopters flying south
Google page sheds leaves

Leaves fall from the trees
Outside the crematorium –
Inside baby sings

Einstein in the cold
Eating ice-cream to keep warm
Relativity

Skating on canal
Not all it's cracked up to be
Disappearing man!

Drops of rain
Fall on my notebook
The poem is written

In the deep dark wood
I photograph you naked
The deer show no fear

The moon is falling
She catches it easily
In her open mouth

This way or that way
Go whichever way you go
All paths leading home

Spire among masts –
What ocean are you crossing
Cassocked helmsman?

Army on the march
If the bugle plays louder
It will wake the dead

As seen through your eyes
I'm unrecognisable
I like the new John!

Return to the start
United in remembrance
Yesterday again!

Seagull bangs on roof
Inviting me to join her
In flights of fancy

Strangers meet
Two minds tussle
Bodies play

Business as usual
When Daleks get religion
Ex-com-mu-ni-cate!

Cut into my face
There is a convenient hole –
Doughnut does not crash

The grass springs up straight
There's no lasting impression
From your fat bottom

Fish doing press-ups
Don't laugh at them
They'll land on their feet!

Five hundred species
Of bacteria in your mouth
Don't spoil this kiss

If all your worries
Could fit inside a haiku
Cock a doodle do!

Pressure cracks his skull
Nobody loves a sailor
With his thoughts exposed

See the plane up high
A Boeing 575
Suspended by words

Invisible words
Just ahead of my pencil
I try to catch them

To the library
Where all my spare heads are kept
Today Basho head!

At the door stood a small man with bright eyes.

"Yes?"

"Hello," he smiled.

"What do you want? Who are you?"

"I am your guru."

He took advantage of my total surprise to bounce into my flat. "I don't need much," he said. "Is there space in the garden for a tent? Of course if you have a spare room so much the better." He opened a door at random and said, "This will do."

"Now just a minute," I spluttered. "What do you mean by barging in? I've never seen you before in my life."

He looked at me calmly, "You read spiritual books, don't you?"

This was true; I nodded.

"Well I'm sure you've come across a wise saying explaining that when the disciple is ready the master will appear."

I nodded again; I had read this and I guess half-believed it.

"Well I have some good news for you: you're ready! I'm going to meditate now; let me know when it's supper time." With that he walked into my spare room and shut the door.

Supper was a strange affair. I couldn't take my eyes off him. Never in my life had I seen anyone eat with so much gusto: there was sucking and smacking of lips, and orgasmic sounds of approval. Part of me was disgusted, but another part envied such unrestrained and uninhibited gastronomic pleasure.

I decided to broach the subject of our supposed relationship. "So when are you going to start teaching me?"

"I am teaching you," he replied, licking his fingers.

"Do you belong to any tradition?"

"Yes, the timeless, spaceless non-tradition."

After supper I googled this, but as I had expected no such

tradition existed.

"If you don't mind," he said, "I'm going to have an early night. It was a long journey."

"Have you come from India?" I asked.

"No, Basildon."

I slept fitfully; I couldn't stop thinking about my uninvited guest. At about 3 a.m. I was on my way to the kitchen for a glass of water, when I noticed the guest room door was ajar and there was nobody in the bed. Then to my great alarm I noticed the door to the apartment was open too. I ran to the living room, but my laptop was still there, as was my prize possession: a Gibson Les Paul once owned by Jeff Beck.

I stood by the door of the apartment wondering what to do. For some unknown reason I was drawn to climb the stairs up to the communal roof garden. At the top I was hit by a blast of cold air. Out on the roof, in the wind and the rain, with his back to me, stood the self-proclaimed guru, in his hand a powerful flashlight.

"What the hell?!" I was astonished. I wanted to know what he was doing, but it felt strangely inappropriate to disturb his "ritual". I watched for a minute as he stood there straight as a lighthouse, a beacon on a stormy night guiding lost souls. Then I left him, went downstairs and got back into bed.

Next morning as the toast popped up the "guru" appeared.

"Did you sleep well?" I asked.

"Very well."

I looked at him intently, but decided not to broach the subject of the night-time roof antics. As we sat having breakfast I tried to create a word description of him in my mind. It wasn't easy, unless "nondescript" counts. Sure, I was sitting opposite a man, but that's all he was: just a man, a generic man, the mere outline of a man. If I tried to look at the detail or guess what was inside, my gaze seemed to slide off and I was left with just the outline.

I spread butter on another piece of wholemeal toast, and then noticed a curious thing. The "guru" was pointing at me. His arm was outstretched across the table and his right index finger was pointing straight at me. Now, in different cultures pointing at someone can mean different things: it can be seen as rude, or a way of cursing someone. But for me in that moment it meant only one thing. The role of the guru was to point directly to the truth. The guru was telling me: I AM the truth. What I'd been searching for all these years was right here. I felt a tingling in my spine.

"You've got jam on your chin," he said.

"Oh!" I dabbed at the spot indicated.

"By the way, you haven't told me your name yet," I said.

He looked me straight in the eye. "Frank," he said, "Frank Lampard." And with that he brushed some crumbs off his shirt and left.

My mood was not helped when a moment later I discovered a copy of *The Observer* sport section right next to his plate.

Work was difficult. I kept on thinking of "Frank Lampard". Well okay, maybe that really was his name. Eventually though, the routine took over. I spent the day playing with Perl code to create a website for a bunch of alternative practitioners. What colour and font size went best with, "YOU CAN CHANGE YOUR LIFE"?

Did I want to change my life? Most people did. Or did I want to be at one with everything just as it was?

When I arrived home I found Frank watching football on TV.

"What you been doing, Frank?"

"I've been looking through your stuff."

"WHAT!"

"Isn't that what every guest does when the host leaves them on their own?"

I was speechless.

"In any case," Frank continued, "how can I truly help you

unless I know more about you?"

"At least," I said, "my laptop is safe from you."

"Oh, it took me about ten minutes to guess your password."

Now I was furious.

"Look," he said, "you want me to hand over the ultimate truth. Surely it's a pretty good deal if in exchange I know a few of your trifling secrets."

"You're not a real guru. A proper guru would treat his followers with respect."

"A proper guru does not consider he has any followers." Frank stood up and added, "What is the right way to behave? Do you think you get handed a manual when you become enlightened? It's about freedom. And you are free to chuck me out. Shall I pack my bags?"

I sat down on the sofa, not knowing what to say.

The buzzer sounded.

"Oh, shit!"

I'd completely forgotten it was Scrabble night. If I'd remembered I would have cancelled it. I pressed the button to unlock the downstairs door. A minute later there was a soft knock. It was Sam, a colleague from work, armed with a well-worn copy of the Collins Official Scrabble Dictionary. Apparently he considered this excellent bedtime reading. He was followed by Charlie and Nancy, a couple living in the same block, who were also Scrabble fanatics. After brief introductions it was decided that I would play Frank, and the others would play a threesome.

Once rearranged, my first rack gave me AEIDHNP. This looked quite promising. Employing a technique I often used of looking for two words I came up with PIN and HEAD. I was pretty sure PINHEAD was valid. Bingo on my first go! Frank came up with a pathetic POP.

My second rack gave me CDEKOOU. Not so promising, but hang on a minute. I saw COOK, then COOKED. Using the N in my first word I had UNCOOKED. Second bingo! The tile fairies were being kind tonight. Frank came up with CON for 14 points, but seemed delighted with his effort.

Already feeling very smug, I examined the letters on my third rack: EIHJNNO. Frowning with concentration I eventually saw JOHNNIE. But was it a valid word? I knew JOHN was valid because it's a term used for a prostitute's customer among other things, but I had never seen JOHNNIE on a Scrabble board. Frank challenged, but Sam found it in his dictionary. This was amazing. This was turning into the best game I'd ever played. Once again Frank put down a three-letter word: GEE in the bottom left-hand corner. I'd won! I was nearly 250 points ahead after only three goes. How could I not win?

The game continued and not surprisingly I couldn't find any more bingos. Then Frank with the same smile he had maintained all along put down ECSTASY.

"Well played, Frank," I said to encourage him.

"Not really," he said, "that's just how the letters came out on the rack: E-C-S-T-A-S-Y. I didn't do anything."

I played my move and Frank calmly put down FREEWOMEN for 101 points, using the E in my first word and the N in CON. I was stunned. He'd been playing so badly. How could he manage to string together two bingos? But was it a word? I knew FREEMAN and FREEMEN were valid, so why not FREEWOMEN? I decided not to challenge. I put down my next word and picking up my tiles realised with surprise the bag was empty. Frank sat staring at his final seven letters, the enigmatic smile still on his face. I noticed the others had abandoned their game and stood looking down at our board. My position had been unassailable; I was still way ahead and bound to win unless...

Frank gave me a look I couldn't decipher and bingoed out with PUZZLER.

Nancy gasped, "That is so cool!"

"Man, what a symmetrical game!" exclaimed Charlie. "Three bingos at the beginning and three at the end. Wow!"

Sam was practically in a state of trance. "The gods have spoken," he intoned solemnly.

"Well done, Frank," I mumbled with enormous difficulty.

"Winning at Scrabble makes me hungry," said Frank. "Any snacks?"

I went to the kitchen and while I prepared the food the others started new games. Frank played Nancy and this time was soundly beaten. I didn't play again that evening. I had totally lost the will to Scrabble. As I rolled an olive around on my plate I tried to bring some order to my thoughts and emotions. Had the "gods" spoken, or was it just randomness playing itself out? According to quantum mechanics, the very next moment I could find myself on Mars. There was nothing in science to say it couldn't happen. It was just incredibly improbable. Things happened, including the improbable sometimes. There was no need to bring in mystical explanations.

I recalled a conversation I had with a priest once. I asked him this question: when faced with a dilemma how can one be sure that a sign from God really is from the divine? He thought about it and said, "Ask for a second sign."

I looked across at Frank. He seemed just as happy losing as winning. I guess a nondual guru would enjoy watching "himself" beating "himself".

When everybody had left Frank and I stood by the rain-swept window.

"What can you see?" asked Frank.

"I see buildings. I see trees silhouetted against the hills. I see the lights of cars."

"What you see is your mind," said Frank. "Goodnight."

That night I slept badly again. The same question kept going round and round in my head: how can one tell if someone is enlightened? In other words, if one meets a guru how does one know if he or she is the real deal?

Did the question even make sense? I was of course aware of the view that enlightenment cannot happen to someone. It's when there is nobody at home that enlightenment is present. And did the answer even matter? When faced with a guru who was suggesting a path (or non-path, as was the latest fashion), one could test it out for oneself. One could decide on the basis of one's own experience the truth or otherwise of the teaching, without regard to the bone fides of the guru. But dammit, I craved a test as definite as litmus!

As a distant clock struck four times I thought I'd found one. At last I managed to sleep.

The next morning when I entered the kitchen Frank was already there, sitting at the table, and still reading the same copy of *The Observer* sport section.

"Listen to this," said Frank. "A defender near the goal line makes a last-ditch attempt to clear a goal-bound volley. He makes a wild swing for the ball, his boot flies off, hits the ball and deflects it behind the goal to safety. You are the ref, what do you do?"

"That's a tough one," I said, "and highly improbable."

"Yes," laughed Frank, "and that's just football. The variety of challenges life throws up is infinite. How can one possibly live according to a schema when there will always be so many unique situations never anticipated by the rules?"

The moment of truth was approaching. I seated myself in front of Frank and breathed in deeply. Let the Guru Test begin.

"Aren't you having breakfast?" enquired Frank. Not bothering to answer I looked at him and made sure I was comfortable and alert. In a moment I would know if Frank was for real. It was going to take a split second, but I had to be sure I didn't miss it.

"Are you enlightened?"

Granted it sounded simplistic, but there was method to my madness. The test depended on whether there was a moment of hesitation between the end of the question and the answer. There were four possible outcomes, which last night I had mapped out using nested IF...THEN statements in the same way I would have done faced with a programming problem at work.

```
IF Hesitation = FALSE Then
        IF reply = "No" Then
                "Person is probably what he/she says, not
                        enlightened"
        ELSE if reply = "Yes" Then
                "No definite conclusion can be drawn"
        END IF
ELSE IF Hesitation = TRUE THEN
        IF reply = "No" THEN
                "Person is almost certainly what he/she says, not
                        enlightened"
        ELSE IF reply = "Yes" THEN
                "Person definitely not enlightened"
        END IF
END IF
```

In other words there was only one outcome where the conclusion was certain, and that was when you asked somebody if they were enlightened and they momentarily hesitated before saying that they were enlightened. They were either lying or fooling themselves.

It was not so much the fact of a gap between the question and answer that mattered, but the "quality" of that gap. One needed to observe it very carefully for a definite case of hesitation as the egoic evaluating mind came in and started calculating the most advantageous way of answering. There might also be the merest flicker of anxiety or worry.

There is a view, of course, that says the enlightened never claim they are enlightened. I didn't think this was necessarily true. In any case my test was not meant to deal with that situation, but only the fourth outcome of the IF...THEN statement.

In response to the question Frank opened his mouth and laughed. Head back, he laughed a continuous shrill laugh for three minutes measured by my TinTin kitchen clock. Dammit, that wasn't one of the expected outcomes (always the fatal flaw with computer programs).

When Frank's merriment had finally run its course our

gazes locked, and neither of us spoke. After a while a memory surfaced. I recalled a talk given by Tony Parsons of "The Open Secret" fame. As I climbed some steps leading up to the building where the talk on nonduality was to be held, I crossed paths with a man coming down. There was nothing in any way remarkable about him and I forgot all about it except that, ten minutes later when the talk started, I was surprised to discover it was the same man appearing on stage. I also recalled the fateful day when a couple of IBM executives called on the fledgling Microsoft company and mistook the skinny lad who let them in for the office junior. They asked to be taken to Mr Gates and he led them to his own office.

"There's something I need to ask you," said Frank. "A favour really."

"Yes, what is it?"

"I'm a bit short. Would you mind lending me twenty quid? I need to buy some toiletries and things."

"Sure, Frank," I said.

"I'll pay you back soon."

"No worries."

At work, the manager called a meeting to discuss the website my team was creating for the alternative practitioners. Apparently they weren't totally happy; they thought the design wasn't "spiritual" enough. They wanted tranquil colours and more crystals.

At coffee time I caught up with Sam (minus his dictionary). Right away he asked how Frank was doing. Frank had been a hit with my friends. I reckoned it was because they'd enjoyed seeing me get my comeuppance at Scrabble. They had no inkling of the guru thing.

That day I had taken the bus to work. On the way home I got off some way from the flat for exercise. As I was walking along the road I was surprised to see a familiar figure coming out of a Ladbrokes betting shop. He crossed over and made straight for a hamburger stand. I knew it only sold meat products and yet Frank had made a point on the first day of insisting he was a strict vegetarian!

He hadn't spotted me. I watched as he paid and turned off towards the municipal park. I carried on home and made straight for the spare room. Without hesitation I opened Frank's travel bag and examined the contents. There were shirts, some underclothes, and a shaving kit. There was the flashlight I had seen him use the first night. There was a notebook. I opened it and was astonished to discover Frank had written about me! There were even verbatim accounts of some of our conversations. This was seriously weird. However, I didn't come across what I had hoped to find, which was a document showing whether Frank was using his real name.

There was one other curious item in the bag. It was a small statue of a woman breast-feeding a child. The figure appeared to be crowned with the horns of a cow. I was no expert, but to me it looked Egyptian.

I put everything back in the bag as I had found it, and made myself a coffee. I stood at the window waiting for Frank and the inevitable confrontation that would ensue.

A short time later I heard Frank arrive and he entered the living room. I spoke, trying to keep my voice as calm as possible. "Frank, there's something we need to talk about."

He looked at me with a childlike expression. "Well that's funny," he said, "that's just what I was about to say to you."

Before I could react he had started.

"Look, I've decided to come clean. That guru stuff is all bullshit. I made it up."

"But why, Frank?"

He shrugged. "I needed to spend time in town to sort out a few things. I can't afford a hotel, or even a B&B."

"But why me? How on earth could you have known I would fall for it?"

Frank grinned. "Can't you guess?" he said. "Where does one find all the information one needs? The Web of course. I looked at social media and sites like www.123people.com. It's all there. I know your job, your previous jobs, where you were educated, the names of your friends and contacts. I know your interests, including the mystical stuff and Scrabble of course."

He chuckled. "Sorry about beating you the other night. I was a semi-finalist in the National Scrabble Championship a few years ago."

"So why are you telling me?" I asked.

He shrugged. "I don't know. Maybe because you're a nice guy. I'll leave right away. I guess you're pretty annoyed with me."

This was true, but what I really felt was deep disappointment.

Frank headed for the spare room.

"Wait," I cried, "there's more we need to talk about."

He stopped and faced the window where I was still standing.

"I found your notebook. What's all that about?"

Frank looked sheepish. "Well, it isn't the first time I've done this," he explained. "I find gullibility interesting, especially when it's connected with religion and spirituality. I might write a book about my experiences one day."

"But that's horrible, Frank. It's taking advantage of people's good nature."

"But, it's so damn easy," exclaimed Frank. "People are desperate to believe. They'll believe anything if you couch it the right way. If I wanted to, I could make a good living by setting myself up as a guru."

"Your world-view is so cynical, Frank," I cried in disgust. "Is there anything you believe in?"

He looked at me seriously for a moment. "Actually there is something I believe in, and given that you've looked in my bag you should know what it is."

"What?" I asked, but he just shrugged.

"Look," he said, "let me give you a piece of free advice. No guru bullshit, just my honest opinion. You seem a sound chap. You've got a flat, a good job and some nice friends. Right now what's wrong with the way things are, just as they are?"

He paused. "Why did you let me in the first day instead of telling me to fuck off? Because you're searching. You're desperately searching and you thought I might help you find what you're looking for. You didn't do it for my sake."

I realised that what Frank was saying was essentially true. I had done it purely for selfish reasons. If Frank had simply said, "I'm a bum with no place to stay," would I have been so hospitable?

"I know you find my table manners disgusting," continued Frank, "but, the way I look at it, there was an eternity in which I ate no pizza. After I die there will be another eternity in which I eat no pizza. My God, if I have a pizza in my hands I'm going to relish it! We have so little time."

"You're starting to remind me of Homer Simpson," I said.

Frank laughed. "Hey, don't knock my favourite philosopher! I'm just about done, but let me say this. You transcendental seekers are fixated on what isn't. You seem to think life is a mistake that has to be put right. What I think is that it's bloody amazing a bunch of atoms have sat up *knowing* they are a bunch of atoms sitting up looking at the sky."

He stopped and sighed. "I'll pack my bag. It won't take long."

Frank Lampard, if that really was his name, stood in the corridor. The posture of his slight frame suggested sadness, but maybe that was just a projection of my own feelings.

"Well, this is it," he said.

"Frank, you never told me what you were doing up on the roof," I said.

"Oh, you know about that? Sorry, but I can't tell you."

After a pause he added, "But if you like, I will tell you what I believe in. You know you asked me earlier."

"Okay, Frank, tell me. What do you believe in?"

"I believe in Isis."

"What!"

"Isis. I-S-I-S."

I remembered the statue. "Isn't that an Egyptian god?" I asked.

"Yes, or rather goddess," he replied. "She's the goddess of life and magic, a friend of the downtrodden and the sinner." He chuckled and added, "A very clever and cunning goddess actually; she tricked Ra into revealing his true name. She is IS-ness."

"And why Isis?"

"My parents were atheists. I was brought up to despise religion. So what better way to rebel against them than by turning into a believer! Trouble was finding the right religion. I didn't care if my religion was true, I just wanted to find one that resonated. But the more I looked into it, the more appalled I became. Basically no religion follows what the founders actually said."

"No wonder you ended up with something weird and unusual," I interrupted. "You're nothing if not one of a kind, Frank."

"We're all one of a kind," said Frank. "Have you ever experienced somebody else's consciousness? All my life I've only ever experienced one consciousness, so I live according to what that tells me."

"Have you ever prayed to Isis and asked her to intercede?" I enquired.

"Never" he said. "If I did that and there was no answer it would destroy my faith. Isis is my last chance saloon. So far I've never needed to call on her, so I live with the hope intact that ultimately, in extremis, succour is at hand."

We shook hands and Frank left. I couldn't think of one thing I felt like doing. I stood by the door as if paralysed. Eventually, pulling myself together, I grabbed my keys and rushed out.

I took the stairs. As I approached the entrance lobby I realised how funny everything was that had happened these last few days. But the funniest thing of all was Frank's cult of Isis. She is IS-ness! By the time I stepped outside onto the pavement I was laughing out loud. Then it struck me like a thunderbolt: *but all my ideas are equally ridiculous!*

It's a terminal case of advanced absurdity. In a timeless moment, all thinking drops away. The town looks the same, but it's an image carved out of Silence.

Up above, a white cloud in a blue sky. I don't see the cloud. I am the cloud. Everywhere I AM to be found. Where is the constricting little vortex that used to be localised in the head? There is only Consciousness without limits.

A woman is passing by. She's transparent. Her veins and bones cannot be seen, but her inner essence shines as Love.

A man approaches and asks for directions. Words come out of my mouth. It's totally effortless. There is such a sense of well-being. Everything is just right by being neither perfect nor imperfect.

There is walking. The body so light. There is hearing the clock strike, but there is no time-keeper.

Why have I never seen this? No, this has always been known. It's home. No explanation comes as to why it was ever less than totally obvious.

A COLD-BLOODED SIGN

There it was. Once more Dickie caught sight of the lizard through the rear window.

"Can't we go faster?" he demanded.

The cabbie raised his hands in exasperation. "I can honk my horn if it makes you feel any better."

Dickie looked back through the morning traffic, but the lizard was gone. They had started appearing some time ago. He felt sure they were after him, but so far he had managed to escape. Not for the first time, he wondered if he was hallucinating, but would an hallucination be so consistent and specific? He punched the seat next to him in frustration. If he tried that with a lizard, would his fist pass right through?

The taxi dropped him off outside an imposing property in Hampstead. Slightly late for his appointment, he was led to a study filled with Biedermeier furniture and antiquities from around the world, but what dominated the room was an impressive couch covered with an oriental rug. An elderly, bearded gentleman with a deep searching gaze entered and indicated to Dickie that he should lie on the couch. Then he seated himself in a chair and remained silent.

"I have a problem," began Dickie.

"I have a problem too," responded the man with an Austrian accent. "I am addicted to cocaine and cigars."

This was not how Dickie had imagined the session. "I see lizards," he said, more emphatically.

"Tell me, what do the lizards do?"

"They chase me."

"Have you considered that they may want to tell you something?"

"I'm too scared to find out, I run away."

The man stroked his beard. "Yes, yes, I see your problem.

You don't know what's worse. Is it to realise that you have a serious mental illness and suffer from hallucinations? Or is it to discover that you are quite sane, but live in a world where reptilian creatures are out to get you?"

Yes, thought Dickie, whichever way you looked at it, it didn't look good.

"By the way," asked the man, "who told you about me?"

Dickie's mouth began to work and then stopped – he couldn't remember. It was most peculiar. "I'm sorry, I don't recall. I think it must have been a colleague at work. Perhaps he was concerned about me because I recently made a mistake and I never make mistakes."

"I never make mistakes," repeated the man chuckling. He lit a cigar. "Please excuse me, it helps me think."

The smell seemed to trigger something in Dickie and he sat up abruptly. "Oh my God! I know who you are! You're Sigmund!"

"Please, address me as Doctor Freud."

"But this is insane. You died over seventy-five years ago!" Dickie began to laugh painfully and hysterically. "I suppose Jung is going to walk through that door next!"

"Ah my prince, he was such a talker that one. Every time he stayed I would have Jungian dreams. Let's try his word association test. Ready?" Dickie nodded.

"LIZARD."

"Dragon."

"DRAGON."

"Mother."

"Interesting," said Freud writing in his notebook.

"Stop, please," shouted Dickie, "we're just playing games! We're not facing up to the main issue of how this can be real!"

"Look," said Freud, "you obviously believe you're having a consultation with me. It is my considered professional opinion, based on years of practice and investigations, but mostly on the fact that I am dead, that you are suffering from a massive hallucination. However, given that I am dead I will waive the fee."

"But that's impossible!" protested Dickie. "It's true I do see the *occasional* lizard, but the rest of my life is all solid. I have a home, a cat, a job. I was driven through the streets of London to get here. There's a whole living city out there."

"Look, there is a simple way to prove whether or not I'm real," said Freud. He puffed vigorously on his cigar. "I'm going to press the lit end of my cigar down on your forehead right here on the brow chakra. Did you know green iguanas and some other lizards have a third eye? You will see, but at a much deeper level."

Before Dickie could protest, Freud was on him. There was a searing light...

...then the next moment a wonderful coolness. A green face looked down on him and removed some medical contraption from his head. It was a lizard's face. Next to him were two Komodo dragons.

"Welcome back," said the lizard, noting something down on his clipboard. "You're well on the road to a full recovery."

"Hello, son," said the first Komodo dragon.

"We've been so worried about you!" cried the second dragon, flicking a yellow forked tongue and clutching her human-skin handbag.

A FUNNY THING HAPPENED ON THE WAY TO THE SUPERMARKET

I locked my flat and started walking towards Morrisons. As I passed the Italian café I was accosted by a middle-aged woman wearing sunglasses, despite a grey sky.

"I'm looking for Cranks," she said.

"Do you mean the vegetarian restaurant?" I asked.

"Yes," she replied.

"Well," I said, "not only are you in the wrong town, but you're also in the wrong time."

"What do you mean?" she asked.

"There was a Cranks in Dartington, a few miles from here, but it closed a while back."

"That's not a problem," she said taking out her mobile phone. It had an unusual design. Maybe it was a new Apple. I wouldn't know, it's not my religion.

"Did you say Dartington? Oh, it's okay, I've found the coordinates. Would you say Cranks was operating there in July 2015?"

"Yes, I think so," I replied, somewhat puzzled.

She punched a number into her unusual phone and promptly vanished.

Astounded, I kept walking round and round the spot where she had stood like a crazy dog, staring at the colour of the pavement, as if that could provide a clue as to where she had gone.

I saw there was an old man with a grizzled beard, wearing shorts and sandals, sitting on a public bench nearby.

"Excuse me," I enquired, "did you see something unusual just now?"

"Yes," he said emphatically.

"What did you see?" I asked eagerly.

"I saw people walking past. If you ask me they're all bloody cranks in this town."

ENLIGHTENED?

Archie: I feel peaceful all the time. There's no striving. No trying. There's nobody seeking. No going hither and thither. Just being *here.*

Krishna [no, not that one]: And when did this start?

Archie: 2015, that's when I had my experience.

Krishna: Hmm, I hate to break this to you Archie, but you're not enlightened.

Archie: I'm not?!

Krishna: How did you feel before the experience?

Archie: So harassed, so stressed. My boss was always on my case. I had the responsibility of supporting my family. There was the long journey to work every day, usually stuck in traffic. It was hell.

Krishna: And do you remember exactly what happened in 2015?

Archie: I told you, I had my experience.

Krishna: Archie, shall I tell you what that experience was?

Archie: What?

Krishna: It was your retirement party. You're not enlightened – you're retired.

Archie: *What!* But, hang on a minute. Why am I peaceful all the time?

Krishna: It's because you no longer have to meet deadlines. It's because your kids have left home.

Archie: But I told you, I'm no longer striving.

Krishna: That's because you've paid off the mortgage with your retirement lump sum.

Archie: But I'm no longer running hither and thither.

Krishna: Why should you? You shop online now and your groceries get delivered to your door.

Archie: No wait, people no longer annoy me!

Krishna: Of course they annoy you, Archie. It's just that your memory has become so poor, you've forgotten the incidents the next day.

Archie: There is something! I used to be troubled by lust and now

I'm not.

Krishna: That's not enlightenment, that's old age. Your gonads have shrunk.

Archie: This is unbelievable. I'm not enlightened, just retired. Are you sure?

Krishna: Quite sure.

Archie: So this means I don't have to write a book about my enlightenment experience.

Krishna: No, you don't.

Archie: That's a relief actually. I was getting really worried about coming up with a good title. All the enlightened teachers around have grabbed the best ones. There's nothing left for me!

Krishna: There you go.

Archie: Hey, this also means I don't have to give talks, or start a Facebook group. It's getting really hard coming up with a fresh way to say what's already been said so many times. For goodness sake how much longer can we go on about the ocean? Surely one day an audience somewhere will start puking when they hear the ocean-wave metaphor.

Krishna: Hahaha!

Archie: But what shall I do instead?

Krishna: You could take up gardening.

Archie: I hate gardening!

Krishna: You can do anything you like.

Archie: Couldn't I just do a little bit of part-time guru-ing, say at weekends?

Krishna: Archie!

Archie: Sorry, Krishna. No, you're right. I can't thank you enough; it's such a relief to drop the idea of being enlightened. I feel so liberated.

Krishna: *ARCHIE!*

A TALE OF TWO CITIES

I throw open the windows and breathe in. The air is fresh because only electric vehicles operate here in the megacity spread out before me. The skyscrapers are beautiful, like fantastic trees grown from seeds originating in the best minds and the best software.

Later, I stroll down the clean, sunlit boulevards, relaxed and happy; crime is unknown here.

I enter a food emporium and browse the shelves, using stepping stones to cross the stream that gurgles through the building. The sound is so much more relaxing than Muzak. All the food here comes from organic farms. There are even wild mushrooms freshly picked from the forest situated on the edge of the city. You just take what you want and walk out.

Back outside I look up into the clear blue sky...

...which is suddenly ripped open and an old woman with a bent back appears shouting, "Johnny, I warned you: no homework, no VR headset!"

I switch on the light. Although it's summertime and four o'clock in the afternoon, it's too dark to read with all the pollution. Outside, the noisy choking city struggles on, and each day the water level rises.

AN ABSOLUTE MARVEL

His new smart phone was an absolute marvel, there was nothing it couldn't do. It monitored his health, it reminded him of his appointments, it warned him if someone approaching had a criminal record.

One day while he waited for a self-driving taxi he amused himself by asking it idle questions.

He asked it, "When will I die?"

The human-sounding, computer-generated voice dropped to a whisper, "Next Tuesday morning at 9:25."

BREXIT-ON-SEA

The family needed a better home. Dad thought he'd found the perfect spot. It had great views, and that was because it was on top of a cliff. Being a democratic family they agreed to vote on whether to leave for the cliff, or to remain in town. They had three children and decided arbitrarily that 12 was the minimum voting age, so their youngest child couldn't vote. Mum argued that the cliff was further from the shops and it would be harder to get food. The son said he wanted to remain in town to hang out with his friends. So those two voted to remain. But Dad, the older daughter and grandma, voted to leave; therefore they went ahead with the purchase. A survey was carried out and contracts exchanged.

At this point there was a shock phone-call from the director of the surveying company. He told them that the surveyor they had sent out (who was no longer with the company) had supplied false information. He advised the family not to go ahead because there was a strong possibility that the house they were planning to move into would crash into the sea!

The family suffered a further setback: that night grandma died in her sleep. But soon after the funeral there was a cheerful event when their youngest child reached her twelfth birthday. Like her brother she felt it would be more fun to stay in town rather than live in isolation on top of a cliff. In the light of all this the mother demanded a second vote. The first time the majority had been in favour of leaving, but now the numbers would be 3 to 2 to remain. The father said no way. He argued, rather badly and paradoxically, that it was undemocratic to vote. He said they had made their decision and must stick to it no matter what.

The mother was astonished, "You mean you want to put the lives of our children in peril by moving to a house that's likely to fall into the sea?!"

"Yes," he replied. "We've signed the initial contract, and put in a lot of time and effort to get this far. We have to stick to our plan. If the house starts to move I'll make you a nice cup of tea and a bacon sandwich."

BRING ME THE HEAD OF DONALD TRUMP

"Happy birthday."

These were the first words he heard. He opened his eyes and took in the neutral blue gaze.

"How old am I?"

"560."

There was a pause, then a delicious wave of joy flooded through him. He had actually survived death! He felt like leaping up and dancing round the room. But the problem was he had no body. He hadn't been able to afford whole body preservation, and only his head had been frozen. But surely after 500 years of progress they would have the technology to provide him with a new body?

Over the next few days they asked him about his life. He told them he had been born in Manchester, where he had graduated in engineering. Later he'd travelled around the world working in fracking. Whenever he could he made use of his Old Trafford season ticket, even if it involved a special flight. He had never married.

He was surprised by some of the trivial questions he was asked, like what kind of cars he had driven. And he was frustrated by their evasive answers to his questions about acquiring a body, meeting others like himself, and exploring the world outside. What he'd taken to be windows were in fact very advanced holograms.

A week after his "re-birth" he had a visitor, obviously someone important from the way the medical orderlies deferred to her. Without introducing herself she told him they were located underground. Then she changed the holographic display to a live feed from the surface. He was shocked. It was nothing like the Earth he knew, and for a moment he was profoundly disoriented.

He wondered whether he was still in the twentieth century having a nightmare, or whether his frozen head had been abducted by aliens and this was their hellish world, looking like some worst-case scenario for the greenhouse effect. Finally, and grimly, she told him that his trial was scheduled to start tomorrow for his part in the greatest crime against the environment.

"Obviously," she said looking down at his head with its spaghetti of wires and tubing, "you were expecting a different kind of reception. Thanks to people like you, I've never seen a living tree."

"What's going to happen to me?"

"Don't worry," she said, "you're small fry compared with the ex-CEO of ExxonMobil we located last month."

CHRISTMAS GHOST STORY

There it was again. It was a scratching sound. Nervously he opened the back door and felt something brush against his leg. He turned and there in the kitchen, as dark as the night, was a large black cat.

It was Christmas Eve, not that one could have known by looking around. There was no Christmas tree, no cards on display, no turkey in the fridge and no wrapped-up presents. But it was an auspicious time and fate had provided him with an unexpected companion. He did not have the heart to throw the animal out into the cold.

When he tried to pick up the cat she hissed ferociously and then proceeded to inspect everything with a strangely proprietorial air, as if the kitchen was her very own domain.

Later the cat joined him where he sat, close to an open fire. He stared into the flames as if the witness of some terrifying scene from the infernal realms.

The grandfather clock rattled for a moment and then proceeded to announce midnight with deep ponderous chimes. It was the first time in ten years that he was not completely alone on Christmas Day. Once he would have been with his wife Yvette, and they would have gone to Midnight Mass and returned to eat bûche de Noël.

Until that fateful night when, in a drunken state, they had decided to stage their own black mass at home. It was meant as a joke – not as the setting for a human sacrifice. It had been a tragic accident of course. Everyone knew that.

The cat opened her mouth wide in a yawn, displaying needle-sharp teeth. She then jumped up, hind legs on his thighs and front paws on his chest. Her piercing blue eyes reminded him of his wife. The cat unsheathed unnaturally long claws and, very gently at first, began to caress his exposed throat.

COUNT YOUR BLESSINGS (AS ME NAN USED T'SAY)

Hell fire, t'were lovely t'day Earth were destroyed. There was no faffin' about, flippin' eck mountains danced and t'sky put on a proper champion display. Mind thee would have liked to stay around a wee bit longer 'fore poppin' me clogs, and less screaming would've been nice, but eee-bah-gom I were chuffed t'bits, t'were reight good – best free show ever!

GASTRONOMIC FALLOUT

My partner was hopeless in the kitchen. When he made chips it sounded like he was chopping down trees. But I didn't care, his cooking was not why I loved him. However, when we decided to live together I realised that actually it was a problem. How could anyone be considered a proper human being if he didn't know about food and spices, and couldn't make delicious meals? I was getting fed up with it. He seemed to spend all his time on his laptop while I worked in the kitchen.

One day I told him that things had to change. He realised I really meant it. The next evening he was still on his laptop, but he had set it up on the kitchen worktop and was looking up recipes. His first attempts were pathetic, but I ate them anyway to encourage him. And I have to say I was pleasantly surprised by his fast progress.

One night I woke up and discovered he wasn't in bed. I found him in the kitchen covered in flour. "Look Suzie, look!" he pointed proudly. In the middle of the night he had been inspired to create a new kind of cake.

He had always had an obsessive personality and now it was applied exclusively to his new passion. It seemed that every day special kitchen gadgets would arrive from Amazon, and when he came back from work his briefcase would be stuffed with spices from the Indian shop and strange-looking fruit and veg.

After a few years I more or less stopped cooking and spent more time in the gym with my friends. One day he told me he had applied to take part in a TV Bake Off programme. I was astonished. I knew he hated being looked at by lots of people, but I was not surprised when he won.

Soon after that we agreed to separate. The last I heard, he had married a chef from one of the top London restaurants.

CRICKET

Human: Cricket cricket.
Cricket: ???
Human: Cricket cricket cricket.
Cricket: ???
Human: Cricket cricket cricket cricket cricket.
Cricket: ???
Human: Cricket cricket.
Cricket: ??
Human: Cricket cricket cricket.
Cricket: ??
Human: Cricket cricket cricket cricket cricket.
Cricket: ??
Human: Cricket cricket.
Cricket: ?
Human: Cricket cricket cricket.
Cricket: ?
Human: <pause>
Cricket: Cricket cricket cricket cricket cricket.
Human: Well done! You've got the hang of addition.
Cricket <via telepathic thought>: My turn now. I'm going to teach the concept of eternity: cricket...

EGO PUNCTURE REPAIR KIT

Have you been told that you're wrong, that you're a failure, or your ideas suck? It hurts doesn't it? But we have the perfect solution. Subscribe to our service today and our trained Ego Puncture Repairers will be there 24/7 to tell you that:

> YOU are right!
> YOU are wonderful!
> YOUR ideas are the best!

Click **Add To Shopping Basket** NOW! Only £25 a month (recurring payment).

Soon suffering from a deflated ego will be a thing of the past. YES you can have an ego AND be happy! Our trained operators are ready to pump you up.

Op: Hello, Ego Puncture Repair Kit.
Customer: I have a complaint.
Op: What seems to be the problem, sir?
Customer: Well today somebody told me I was talking rubbish and my ego was badly deflated, so I phoned the special number and instead of being told I was right your operator started insulting me!
Op: This is most unusual, sir. I do apologise. Could I please have your user ID so I can check the details.
Customer: Yes, my ID is PinkFluffyEgo.
<Music>
Op: I've just checked your details and it seems you haven't paid this month. Your credit card was rejected. So I'm going to have to ask you to get off the line you fucking wanker. You dickhead.
Customer: What?! I –
Op: Hop it you loser, you sad dumbass.

EVERYWHERE AND NOWHERE

I awake with a splitting headache. The place where I am is both familiar and unfamiliar. There is a huge filing cabinet and when I examine it I find it's filled with memories, including an old photograph of my visit to the Centre Pompidou in Paris.

I drift outside and find a pair of familiar-looking legs strolling across the wet grass. I follow until I see a small object. I realise it's a nose. I pick up the nose, but when it sniffs at me I quickly set it down.

I look up and see billions of stars in the daylight sky. They are joined together by filaments that sparkle with electrical excitation. The constellation of Anterior Cingulate Cortex is particularly active. I notice that my changing thoughts match the changing patterns of light above. When I centre myself on the sacred sound OM the sky becomes one vast mandala.

Back inside I notice that the sofa is covered with veiny skin and is hairy in places. On it there's the current edition of *New Scientist* open at page 27 with a sentence about quantum coherence underlined: "This is what allows quantum objects to split their existence, characteristics and properties between spatial locations, different kinds of movement or even between different particles entirely."

I approach the large mirror on the wall, but there is no time for reflection, and no self looks back at me. I return to the filing cabinet which is covered with barnacles hitching a ride across eternity. In the top drawer there is a file, and in the file a mostly accurate record of everything that has just happened, including the fact that I am about to close the top drawer – which I do.

I begin laughing. The laughter stays resonating in the space I had occupied as I drift away, free of everything...

But actually I'm not going anywhere. It's only vection; like the illusion of moving while sitting in a train and seeing another train outside the window. The scenery shifts as smoothly as an elegant albatross skimming the waves of reality, but pure existence remains absolutely still.

GRUMPY GURUS TO STRIKE

It's been announced there'll be a world-wide guru strike next week. All pujas and satsangs will be cancelled, and all pointers to the Truth dismantled and put into temporary storage. The strike is a protest against the lack of respect shown to spiritual teachers nowadays.

A spokesperson for AUGUST (Amalgamated Union of GURus and Spiritual Teachers) was reported as saying, "The strike is regrettable but necessary. Quite frankly, questions during satsang are getting too hard to answer. Seekers should remain in respectful silence and stop complaining about the fees being charged. Can a price be put on Truth?"

A spokesperson for GODASS (Guild Of Devotees And Spiritual Seekers) said she was disappointed that the gurus were setting such a poor example. She is advising her members not to panic.

Richard Dawkins commented on his blog that it will be good for the people affected to depend on themselves for a change and to stop looking to external authority. He added that, as the Pope of Science, he was more than willing to lead them to a better place, where truth was put through the mangle and evidence-based.

A special helpline is being setup for anyone suffering severe guru withdrawal symptoms.

HECK OF A SLOW CHECKOUT

Busy today in Morrisons. I'm looking for the best queue and the search algorithm isn't easy. You can't just go by the number of people. Baskets or trolleys? Loaded? Age of shoppers? Are they going to chat and spend ages fumbling for their purse? Is the cashier dopey, bored, alert, friendly?

I end up behind a man whose diet seems to consist mostly of brown ale. After only a short time I'm entering a trance, only just managing to stave off death from boredom in this insipid place.

But surely something is wrong? It's so slow! In fact this queue isn't moving at all. I exchange a quick glance with the beer man, then notice that the cashier is twiddling his thumbs. Where's the shopper? I remember it was a tall woman wearing a parka. Has she gone off looking for something she forgot? That's so inconsiderate.

The beer man consults his chunky sports watch.

What's happened to her? I'm getting a strange feeling that the tall woman is never coming back. Maybe she's received an urgent call, or been bludgeoned to death with a frozen leg of lamb in the meat section.

"Tssst!"

I'm brought out of my reverie by the sound of a beer can opening. To my enormous surprise he offers me one. But I guess it's part of the human condition to want to share in a crisis.

"What's happened to us?" he says in a thick voice. "Once upon a time we were a band of hunters sprinting across the savannah, todgers girded, spears ready – wildebeest, antelopes, gazelles!"

Wondering how much alcohol he's already had that day, I decide not to mention I'm a vegetarian, though there's a clue in the abundance of avocados in my trolley.

We clank beers in brotherhood.

SECOND STOMACH

"You're joking!" I exclaimed.

"No, it's true," confirmed the car salesperson.

"You mean I'll never have to buy petrol again?" I asked.

"That's right," she said, "this car runs on your leftovers. Just empty the contents of your brown caddy into this receptacle here. The car will do the rest."

I was sold. The money I would save! It was amazing.

The first week went really well, and I had great fun driving my new car. True, it did produce a rather bizarre smell that attracted all kinds of creatures, including seagulls, but the thought of never having to drive into a petrol station again more than made up for it.

It was the second week that the problems began. I was on my way to Torquay for a meeting when the car stopped on the A385. Nothing I tried would get it going again. Thankfully the breakdown chap arrived fairly quickly.

"Any idea what's wrong?" I asked, after he'd had a good look.

"Yes," he said. "I think I've located the problem. It's the engine. Your car is suffering from severe indigestion."

"What!"

"I'm afraid it's not that uncommon with this new type of engine. They are quite delicate, you know."

"They didn't say anything about that when I bought it," I grumbled. "But can you fix it?"

The recovery man stroked his chin. "It's not that simple," he said. "First thing is, you won't be able to use the car for a couple of days. It needs to undergo a cleansing fast. Then after that you'll have to feed it the following foods."

He wrote down a list of items in what looked like a doctor's prescription pad. "This should do it," he said, tearing out a sheet.

I read the list with growing incredulity. "Where am I going to get specialist dishes like these?" I spluttered.

"You're in luck," he replied. "There's a luxury organic health farm not far from here. I'm sure the kitchen staff will supply you with all your requirements. I'll tow you there. And don't forget it's only for a short time while your car is recuperating, then it's back to leftovers."

My plan to save money was turning into a complete fiasco. Getting my car back on the road to health was going to be expensive.

When I finally arrived home I fortified myself with coffee and hot buttered toast, quite satisfied for the first time in my life with the simplicity and complete ineptitude of my toaster.

KEEP OFF THE GRASS

Two appeared before One.

"Ah, I've been waiting for you," said One.

"Sorry," said Two, "but I don't like to come too often in case I disturb you."

"Nothing can disturb me," said One. "Look at this."

There was an object. It was long, thin, and green. They both looked at it.

"Hmm," said Two. "What is it?"

"I call it a blade of grass."

"Is there just the one?" asked Two.

One laughed. "Hardly, look!" He showed Two something else.

"What is it?" asked Two.

"I call it a universe."

"Big, isn't it?"

"Yes," said One.

"What's it for?"

"It's where the grass comes from."

"Oh," said Two.

"Pick any galaxy," instructed One.

Two hesitated.

"Go on. Any one of those." He indicated some spiralling objects.

"OK. That one," said Two.

"Good. Now pick any star."

Once again, by means of pointing, One helped Two understand the meaning of star.

"All right, I'll have that one," said Two, pointing to a small, yellow star.

"Fine. Now you have to pick a planet, but this time it has to be a planet that is just right. Let's see if you can guess which one it is."

Two was starting to get the hang of things. He counted

eight planets, but which one was just right? He plumped for the middle one.

"Too cold," said One.

He tried the second one from the star.

"Too hot," said One.

He tried the third planet.

"Just right!" said One. "Now, what do you see?"

There were many things to see, but Two had only ever seen one of them before.

"I see lots and lots of grass," he said.

"Yes," said One proudly. "Wherever you go in the universe you will find grass. Look along the edge of the sand, look in the cracks in the rocks. It's vulnerable, yet it's tough. It's really admirable stuff."

Two noticed something else. "Those things are eating your grass," he said.

"Those things are called herbivores," said One.

"Oh, but those herbivores are not eating the grass."

"They are not herbivores, they are people. They do not eat this sort of grass. They walk on the grass. They sit on the grass. They cut the grass and put it into bags."

"Can't you stop them?" asked Two.

"Nothing can stop them. Even if you display signs saying 'Keep off the grass', they just ignore them."

"What are people for?" asked Two.

"They are not for anything," explained One. "I created the universe in order to make grass, but you arrived late. So I let the experiment run on. Many things have sprung up."

"I see," said Two. "Well, thank you for showing me your grass."

When Two had left, One watched the grass growing. Not a *single* blade in the whole universe went unnoticed.

Three appeared.

"Ah, Three. Time to tidy up my creation-room, I think."

Three hummed as he worked. Using a huge broom he swept up the universe and dumped it at the back where it wouldn't be noticed.

LANDSCAPE WITH THE ALIEN

Today I explored the planet for the first time. I took only my hat for protection against the fierce sun and a stick to test the terrain. I already knew from my orbital observations that what looked like rivers were actually huge snakes. I was walking nonchalantly next to a blue snake about fifty miles long, confident it had no idea of my presence.

As I passed them, the trees and long grasses bent away from me, as if wishing to avoid all contact with the alien. Because, yes, I was the alien here; this world might feel utterly strange to me, but it possessed its own natural order.

In the distance were miles and miles of what looked like mounds of sand. Later I would discover that they were actually old snake skin, accumulated over millions of years and dried to raw umber under the sun.

Paradoxically the strangest sight of all was three swans hitching a ride on the back of the snake, like oxpeckers on a rhino. Strange precisely because they looked exactly like Earth swans, and so out of place in this extraordinary landscape.

As I looked at them it seemed to me that they were throwing stern looks in my direction and questioning my presence: "Who is this stranger? This is not his home."

I SEE

It was a small, grey gallery and inside was the most extraordinary painting I'd ever seen. I wanted it so badly; however, it was way beyond my means.

I left the gallery empty-handed, but with the best pair of eyes I'd ever had.

MOTHER OF GOD

Mother of God: Oh, my God – so much sex! Why couldn't you create a nice universe like your brothers and sisters?

God: But mother, their universes are so boring! Just pretty patterns of pure energy. Mine has juice.

Mother of God: But it's so dishonest! It's a trick! One minute your creatures think they're having fun, and the next they're changing nappies and worrying about the mortgage. Oh my! That insect is eating its mate while copulating! That's sick, God, really sick!

God: But mother, variety is the spice of life.

Mother of God: Who says?

God: Some people on a little blue planet.

Mother of God: And what do they know, being a part of your twisted plaything?

God: At least my universe isn't like Uma's; it's just a shopping mall that fills the whole of space-time.

Mother of God: I'll have you know that every single shop in that infinite mall sells something different. That is an amazing act of creation. She had to invent a whole new branch of mathematics.

God: It's rubbish.

Mother of God: I'm going to have a word with your father!

God: Mother, how many times do I have to remind you that I'm my own father.

Mother of God: Oh you are cruel; you know it brings on my migraine when you talk like that.

God: I know Mother, I can feel it; after all, I'm my own Mother too.

NOT-KNOWING

Neola: Thank goodness you're here!

Agent: What's up, Neola?

Neola: I know!

Agent: Know what?

Neola: You don't understand: *I know!*

Agent: But you can't mean –

Neola: Yes, I can!

Agent: But *who* knows?

Neola: Don't start that stuff on me before I've even had my first coffee. There is KNOWINGNESS!

Agent: But I've just had hundreds of leaflets printed for Saturday's meeting. They all say you don't know! That's why you're famous: you're the teacher who doesn't know anything. This is a disaster!

Neola: I know.

Agent: But how? How did this happen?

Neola: I thought I knew nothing. I thought I was nothing. Then this morning I woke up and suddenly something rose up from the depths... and I knew.

Agent: Couldn't you stop it?

Neola: How? It just happened spontaneously, and now there's a deep lack of doubt.

Agent: Maybe tomorrow you'll wake up and it will all be forgotten.

Neola: You don't understand. Knowing, forgetting, are all to do with thoughts, but this knowingness is deeper than that.

Agent: But this is awful! Your books, your website, and your talks, they're all about not-knowing. Now all I can think of is that stupid catch-phrase, "She knows you know."

Neola: I'm really sorry; I didn't mean for this to happen.

Agent: Mmm, couldn't you pretend you don't know? Just to buy us more time.

Neola: How could you suggest such a thing!

Agent: Sorry, I'm feeling desperate. So, what shall we do?

Neola: I don't know.

NOW, LISTEN CAREFULLY

"Now, listen carefully. I shall say this only once."

We sat in silence, our attention absolute. We were the lucky ones, chosen by fate backed by faith. We were about to be told, not the ultimate answer to the ultimate question, because that cannot be uttered, but instead a surefire way to know it for oneself. After thousands of years of human endeavour, a teacher had finally stumbled upon a simple *Way* guaranteed to work in a short time.

"What I am about to say must never be repeated. Remember, you have all taken a solemn vow."

The eyes of the little old woman on stage, dressed in a green tweed jacket, seemed to give off a brilliant light. Nobody knew her name. She had been living as a recluse on a remote Scottish isle for over fifty years. She was about to deliver one sermon, and then disappear forever.

I recalled the strangest Facebook message I had ever received. It had to be some kind of phishing attempt, or a joke. But there was no link to click on, and no request for personal information. I was one of a small number who had been chosen at random, and one of an even smaller number who had decided to act on the message. And now I was about to be free forever.

"There are three steps. Step number one –"

A mobile went off near me. How could someone with such an obnoxious ringtone be attending a meeting like this?!

"...and so as you can see, step one is really very simple."

"What did she say?" I whispered to my neighbour.

"Shhh!"

"Now, step number two –"

A baby behind me started wailing. I strained to understand the speaker, but my hearing isn't that good. How inconsiderate of a mother to bring her child to such a momentous meeting! I could feel panic rising, but maybe I could work out the first two steps myself from the final one?

I looked around the room anxiously, but all seemed quiet

now. Everyone waited expectantly.

"Finally, step three –"

What was that?! It sounded like someone tramping across the roof! Then I heard squawking and wailing. It was a squabble of seagulls. By the time I had stopped attending to my anger, it was all over. The little old woman from the Shetland Isles had left the hall.

I groaned in frustration. To have been so close to salvation, and then for it to be snatched away by noise of all things!

I confess that as we all left the hall I approached several people and begged them to share the secret doctrine, but they just looked at me with pity in their eyes. When I (Nudge Nudge Wink Wink) hinted there might be something in it for them, their look of pity turned into one of complete disdain.

And so it was that I began my journey home, bound for Paddington Station, feeling lonely and most decidedly unliberated. But I wasn't alone. Sitting next to me on the tube train was the teacher! I had been so engrossed in my suffering that I hadn't recognised her, or even noticed the green tweed jacket.

I immediately launched into my story and poured out my feelings of loss and disappointment. She listened to everything with attention, but of course she already knew exactly what it was I wanted.

"But if you, then why not the next person? Where does it end? You may see me as a teacher, but unlike Jesus, Ramana and Krishnamurti, that is not my fate. Today I carried out my sacred duty. The seeds of knowledge have been scattered. What happens next is no longer my business."

She sensed my deep disappointment and sighed, "Look, you can have this."

I saw that, in her hand, she held a key.

"What is it?"

"It's the key to my house on Fair Isle. I won't be needing it anymore. By the way, do you play a musical instrument?"

Puzzled, I replied, "Yes, the violin."

"Perfect!"

Living on a remote island, eating fish and making music with the locals, was not what I wanted. "But it took you fifty years, and I'm already older than that!"

She laughed, "I spent too much time photographing the flying migrants. But in any case, having attended this meeting, you have an advantage."

"What advantage? I didn't hear anything."

"But you know one thing. Surely you noticed the brevity of the meeting? You suffered the misfortune of just a few short sounds drowning out the entire teaching. When I started my search I read long, complicated books; and entertained long, complicated thoughts. But that's not *it* – and you know that."

The tube train stopped at Edgware Road and she got off, but not before she had given me the key.

OBSESSION

Bob had a strange obsession. He searched for shells with unusual markings on beaches all over the world. One day he found a shell covered with what looked like the characters of an ancient script. The problem was identifying the language. Bob spent hours and hours examining and photographing his shell, looking for a possible match with the scripts of the Sumerians, Ancient Chinese, and other civilisations.

Bob believed that by this means God had left an important message embedded in his creation, awaiting discovery by the human race. Admittedly it sounded a bit far-fetched, but Bob was convinced that God enjoyed setting puzzles.

Finally, after many years of patient effort, he found a match and managed to decipher the message on his special shell. He was astonished by what it said. It was so much more personal than he could have ever imagined.

Dear Bob

I wish to communicate something of extraordinary significance.

Love, God

P.S. The rest of this message can be found on another shell somewhere on Earth.

OMVILLE

I had assumed it was a track leading nowhere, but coming round a corner I saw a small township. The sign said OMVILLE. I drove down its only street and was pleasantly surprised to discover a café open for business. The menu assured me that everything served here was 100% organic and gluten-free. I ordered a black coffee and a slice of carrot cake, which was brought over by a friendly young waitress.

I looked around; everything was made of chunky wood. There were about half a dozen other customers and I had the distinct impression they were interested in me, but trying not to be too obvious about it.

Then a very fit-looking, middle-aged man with a pleasant open face left his companions and approached me. "Hi there," he said, "you okay?"

"Fine," I said.

"You sure?"

"Quite sure," I replied, a little puzzled.

"Oh," he seemed disappointed. "That's good then," he added without much enthusiasm.

He turned to go back, then changed his mind. "I saw you drive in. Driving can really do your back in. See my friend over there? That's Wally. He's brilliant at backs. He could fix you."

"My back is fine," I assured him.

"Oh, okay."

I focused on my carrot cake, which was fresh and moist, and not at all sickly like the ones you find in supermarkets. The coffee was good too. I looked up to discover a handsome woman in her sixties sitting right next to me. She'd approached so quietly I hadn't even noticed.

"Hello," she said. "Had any interesting dreams recently?"

"I'm afraid not," I informed her, "unless you count the one

where my trousers fell down."

Her eyes lit up and she took out a notebook from her coat pocket.

"Look," I said, "I don't feel comfortable discussing my dream life in public."

"Of course not," she said. "Let's go to my treatment room."

"I'm afraid I have other plans."

"But there's a special introductory discount."

"Sorry, not interested."

"I can help you," she insisted.

"So can I!" piped up Wally from across the room.

"But I don't need any help!" I almost shouted.

From the shocked looks I received it was quite clear that this was just about the worst thing I could have uttered. Everyone turned away and went back to quietly discussing obscure therapies.

I paid and left, deciding before heading off to take a stroll down the street of this rather unusual town. Despite the fact it all looked very clean and tidy, there were many things that seemed in need of repair. Eventually I was back where I had parked my car by the café. The waitress who had served me was sitting outside in the sun having a break.

"Excuse me," I said, "can you tell me about this place?"

She smiled sweetly. "Omville is great. I've lived here all my life. Everyone is so caring and very talented."

"What kind of jobs are there for people around here?"

"Well we have dream therapists, hypnotherapists, psychotherapists, yoga teachers, nutritionists, homoeopaths, acupuncturists, and someone does clown therapy on a Tuesday."

I laughed, "My goodness, you must all be incredibly sane and healthy!"

She nodded, a look of boredom on her perfect, unblemished face.

PIZZA DELIVERY

There was no possibility of going for a stroll that day. The alien had accidentally transported one of my legs into another dimension. Thankfully it didn't hurt.

"I'm so terribly sorry," he said for about the tenth time, using his translation gadget. "What can I do to make it up to you?"

"Nothing," I replied sulkily.

"But our civilisation is so much more advanced than yours, surely there's something I can offer you?"

"Okay then, tell me where everything comes from."

"You mean like the meaning of life?"

"Yes," I said, "I want to know everything."

The alien settled down on his five legs and began. "It all started with emptiness. In fact if you ask me there was too much emptiness, but something happened –"

He was interrupted by the loud chime of the doorbell. It was the pizza delivery boy.

After he had left, the alien asked, "Shall we eat or shall I continue to explain where everything comes from, including time; whether God exists; the nature of the multiverse; how many dimensions there are; and why the fine structure constant is exactly 0.007297351?"

I thought about it for a moment. "Let's eat," I said. "I'm famished."

POOR FING!

I am five years old when I arrive in England. I enter my new school knowing only two words of English.

The other children crowd around to inspect me: they have never seen a French boy before. I want to disappear.

One boy smiles at me. He will become my best friend. His name is Paul Finn. What a lifesaver for a Poor Fing like me.

PORRIDGE PANCAKES PARADOX

My story is set in the Emirates Stadium, the home of Arsenal Football Club. Now I'd like to introduce you to one of the main characters. Her heart is kept in a refrigerator. Each morning experts arrive to tune-up her voice, so as to hide its latent shrillness. She is a politician loved by TV manufacturers, because viewers throw objects at the screen. You don't have to be a detective to know that she killed society with a dagger in the conservatory. My second character is much more believable. Her name is Goldilocks. When she was a little girl Goldilocks had a life-changing experience. I'll tell you what happened.

She was wandering in a forest when she came across a house. She walked right in. Someone was giving a party political speech on behalf of the Communists.

"Too left," said Goldilocks.

She walked into the next room and found a character, with a swastika tattooed on his shaved head, giving a speech on behalf of the Neo-Nazis.

"Too right," said Goldilocks.

She moved into a third room and there she found the Dalai Lama sitting on a meditation cushion, speaking about the Middle Way.

"Just right," said Goldilocks happily.

"Little girl, would you like some porridge?" asked the Dalai Lama kindly.

"Yes, please," said Goldilocks.

Just then Maggie, the wicked witch, appeared and stole all the milk from the fridge.

"Sorry," said the Dalai Lama, "the porridge will have to be made with water and salt only."

So now we come to the main story which is happening, as I've mentioned, inside the Emirates Stadium. Taking up the whole of the hybrid natural grass pitch there's a splendid picnic going on. Everybody is there and Coldplay is providing the music. Goldilocks is sitting next to Thierry Henry and Mrs Thatcher.

Arsène Wenger passes by, carrying a mountain of pancakes. Arsenal has lost one too many matches against Barcelona so now he works for the Emirates catering department.

"I'll have 321," says Mrs Thatcher.

"You won't be able to eat all those!" giggles Goldilocks.

"I will eat them," retorts Maggie. "I will destroy these pancakes. There won't be a single morsel left on my plate. Those expecting a U-turn will find the lady's not for turning!"

Everyone watches her scoff pancake after pancake. But eventually she's struggling. Goldilocks begins to feel sorry for her, even though it was Mrs Thatcher who gave her spindly legs by depriving her of milk.

Now Maggie is perspiring; shedding tears of effort, she battles on with heroic mastication and patriotic swallowing. Her face has taken on a sickly green tinge, but she will not give up. Arsène stands by, a solicitous look on his face; he knows what it feels like to suffer. Turning to a TV reporter he gives this summary: "I believe Madame Thatcher's spirit is 100 per cent, but it's difficult to win against pancakes away from home, especially when one's already conceded two chicken legs. But I cannot question her desire or commitment at all."

Thierry chips in, "When I played on this pitch I wanted to score great goals just as much as Madame Thatcher wants to win here today."

"We human beings won't let anything get in the way of our desires," muses Goldilocks as she watches Maggie sprinting towards the goalmouth of her ultimate achievement.

But just before Maggie can swallow the last pancake, Goldilocks snatches it off the plate, rolls it into a little football, and kicks it out of play. "BITCH!" she cries.

RE-CURSE

He had a special place to write: it was a practically empty room at the top of the house. There was a table, a chair, and a view of wooded hills through the sash window. There was nothing particularly special about the table and the chair; it was a black office chair with plastic armrests, and a rather hideous Formica-top table. But it had to be that table, that chair, and those hills. Quite often the characters in his stories sat at a similar table, on a similar chair; and the action (whether it was a conversation or a murder) took place while out on a similar wooded hill.

On the wall there was a large photograph he had taken; it showed the table, chair, and hills through the window. He was a good photographer and had managed to balance the indoor and outdoor light. When he was not in the room it was an accurate copy of the room it was in, but when he sat on his chair there was a discrepancy of course. However, sometimes at particular times of the day, when the sunlight reflected off the glass of the picture frame, it seemed to create the illusion of a ghostly figure sitting in his chair.

There was one other thing in the room, and that was a dehumidifier. He kept it on low because he didn't like the sound, but even when it was going full blast it never seemed able to remove a nasty, musty smell from the room.

He was sitting in his special place in the house, with a pad and pen, but not actually writing. He was staring at the hills, waiting to know what came next in his story.

The two main characters, Thelma and Jim, had just had an intense argument whilst out for a walk on a hill near their home. They had both run out of words, and he too had run out of words. He was the author and yet he didn't have a clue what was next.

Something unexpected needed to happen to shock all three out of their stasis. He felt that whatever it was it needed to happen in their home, so he walked them back to their three-storey Victorian house, and got Jim to make a pot of tea, in the hope this might soothe Thelma. He then wrote in his pad:

> As soon as Thelma and Jim sat down, they were startled by
> the sudden loud noise of a large bird crashing into the window.

As he made the full stop at the end of the sentence, there was a sudden loud noise as a large bird crashed into the window.

"Wow, that's an *amazing* coincidence!" he thought, already planning how he would write it up on his Facebook page. But for now he needed to focus on the story. He wrote:

> "Do you have any idea how hurtful your words were earlier today?" uttered Thelma.
> "I didn't mean it," replied Jim. "It was said in the heat of the moment. Don't give words such power."
> "Heat of the moment? Well, given it was a cold, October afternoon, your rage must have been incandescent!"

What was that smell? For once it didn't smell musty. He put down his pen and started walking towards the door. It smelt like smoke. He opened it and stood there, paralysed with shock and horror. The house was on fire!

SECOND COMING

Jesus: Any progress?

Lawyer: Nope.

Jesus: But the court case has been dragging on for years! I should never have listened to you. I should have accepted that my words had been misrepresented and left it at that. But you said we should sue all the Christian religions, and then I could use the money to advertise my second coming.

Lawyer: But Jesus we've been through this so many times. You know how it irks you that they got some of your parables wrong, and quoted things you never actually said. Like, "No man cometh unto the Father, but by me." And don't forget they gave Judas, your best buddy, a bum rap.

Jesus: Yeah, yeah, okay. So no change?

Lawyer: Well, I didn't want to bring this up, you've got enough on your plate coping with all us sinners, but I'd better mention it. You agreed to delay the official opening of your second coming until the legalities are ironed out, but various reports have come out saying you're planning to go on the *Oprah Winfrey Show* to set the scene.

Jesus: Yes, so?

Lawyer: Well, various fundamentalist Christian groups have got together and started a counter-claim. They want to obtain a gagging order. They're worried what you might say on the show. They say they already know the Word of God, because it's in the Bible.

Jesus: But for God's sake, I AM GOD!

Lawyer: They believe every word in there is sacrosanct and cannot be changed.

Jesus: But it's full of mistakes. I should know, I was there – and I still have the scars to prove it!

Lawyer: We'll fight it of course.

Jesus: But are you seriously telling me there are people out there who would put the writings in a dusty old book above the living truth coming directly from the lips of their Saviour?

Lawyer: I'm afraid so.

Jesus: But I might want to change my teachings. Freshen them up a bit. Make them more eco-friendly.

Lawyer: That makes them very, very nervous. These people hate change.

Jesus: I guess now I know how Dylan felt when he walked on stage with a Stratocaster and sang about Maggie's Farm being connected to the electric grid.

Lawyer: Yeah, something like that. By the way, I had a call from our security company. They recommend doubling the number of bodyguards.

Jesus: Oh no, I'm starting to get a terrible feeling of déjà-vu...

REFLECTION

Although it was my first visit to Brussels I found the house relatively easily. He opened the door himself, dressed as immaculately as I had expected.

"I have your item from Sotheby's," I said.

He invited me in with great politeness, but as I passed him in the hallway he gave me an enormous kick up the backside, all the while continuing to talk as if nothing had happened. In shock, my eyes smarting from the pain, I asked for the bathroom.

In the bathroom I glanced in the mirror and found, to my horror, I could see the back of my head.

When I emerged he was examining the proof of delivery document. He slipped it into his pocket and shook my hand. Then he let himself out of the front door, and I found myself alone in the hallway.

I heard a voice calling from the sitting-room and went in.

"Another cup of coffee?" asked Madame Magritte.

SOMETHING ROTTEN

It was just an apple tree.

"Urgh!" said Adam. "There's a worm in this apple."

"Urgh!" said Eve. "There's a worm in my apple too."

They both spat out in disgust.

"What a way to treat us!" exclaimed Eve. "We're special, the only human beings in existence."

"Yeah, let's tell God," said Adam.

God listened patiently while Adam and Eve complained about the worm-eaten apples and many other things.

"This garden," said Adam, "it's a bit small, isn't it?"

"Yeah," added Eve, "and how do we *know* it's Paradise? What have we got to compare it with? We've never been on a holiday!"

"That's right," said Adam, "I bet there are places tons better than this." He pointed beyond the Gates of Eden.

"Over there," said Eve, "there's shopping malls and iPods and –"

"What are you blathering on about, Eve?" interrupted Adam.

"Dunno, Adam. Suddenly got all these funny ideas in my head."

"Well," said God, "you don't have to stay, it's up to you."

"We're going," said Eve. "We've had enough of your garden, your worms and your patronising attitude. I expect we're just amusing lumps of clay to you."

"Goodbye then, my children," said God. "Safe journey. Oh, and don't forget to invent clothes. The wind gets bitter out there this time of year."

Adam and Eve opened the Gates of Eden and entered the immense unknown. They walked in silence. After a few minutes doubts began to surface in Adam's mind and turning to Eve he said, "Do you think we did the right thing?"

"Dunno. We'll see. Anyway, it's an adventure!"

STICKING WITH WHAT YOU KNOW

"Where do you come from?"

"Totnes."

"No, I mean when did you start?"

"When I was born."

"So was there a time when you weren't, and then suddenly you knew, 'Here I am!'?"

"No, I don't actually recall a moment like that."

"And how does that make you feel?"

"I guess it's kind of odd that existence just crept up on me, and that I have no recollection of such a momentous event."

"And when you die, will you know that your existence has come to an end?"

"No, death will prevent that."

"So here you are, but without a proper beginning or a proper ending. Is that so?"

"Yes, I have no experience of ever having started, and can never have an experience of not being present."

"So that means —"

"I am."

THAT'S NOT WHAT I ORDERED!

"That's not what I ordered! I'm a vegetarian. I don't eat fish."

"Some vegetarians eat fish," responded the waitress.

"Not real vegetarians," he retorted. He was incensed by her tone. Surely an apology was due? "Bring me what I ordered!" he said loudly.

While he waited he checked Facebook. There were a couple of Likes for his new cover photo, but not as many as he was expecting.

The waitress returned and placed a plate in front of him. He could not believe his eyes.

"WHAT?" he exploded. "But it's fish again!"

"It looks like fish," said the waitress, "but it's not really fish."

"What do you mean?"

"The chef is very talented and creative. She's made you what looks like a fish, but actually is all vegetables and grains."

"But I didn't order fish. I don't want to see anything that might even remotely remind me of fish. I demand to see the chef!"

"Sir, I don't think that's a very good idea," said the waitress.

"You heard me. I demand to see the chef right now!" he repeated.

A few minutes later a figure appeared with the legs of a woman, but the head of a fish. The reverse mermaid was wearing a toque.

"What seems to be the problem, sir?"

THE ALTERNATIVE ELEPHANT STORY

One day a group of blind men on a journey came across something in their path.

The first man felt its tail and said, "I think we must be outside the gates of a palace. I can feel the bell pull."

"Let me see," said another. He went forwards and felt the tip of a tusk. "Oooh, I think you're right. I nearly cut myself on the sword of one of the guards on duty."

Another tried and felt a leg. "My, my, what an impressive column. This must indeed be a fine palace."

And yet another was able to confirm their conclusion when he happened to feel the ear, which he supposed was a large fan being carried by one of the Maharaja's attendants. This continued until all the blind men were satisfied.

By now they were all in a jovial mood. "How fortunate for us to stumble upon this impressive palace," said one. "We must tell our relatives about it when we get home," said a second. "But what a pity the Maharaja is not about, or he might have invited us in for a cup of tea," said a third.

Just then, mocking laughter was heard. Another man had arrived. "You silly old coots," he cried. "There is no palace here. You're standing by an elephant!"

"What nonsense!" cried the blind men. "We have all investigated the matter and are in full agreement."

"And anyway," added one, "why should you know any better?"

"Because my eyes work, that's why," said the newcomer. "I can see."

"It's easy for you to say that," said one of the blind men, "but why should we believe you? You may be a liar. In fact I suspect you are just as blind as the rest of us, but you are a smart fellow. You have heard us talking and with your quick wits have worked out a way to trick us. I bet you are going to say that the bell pull is an elephant's tail and the guard's sword is a tusk!"

The blind men fell about laughing. At that moment another man appeared, who in fact was an enlightened sage. He asked politely what was going on. One of the blind men explained the situation, and then added, "Sir, you sound like a courteous and sensible man, pray settle the matter for us. What are we standing by: a palace or an elephant?"

"Or is it a boat yard?" piped up one of the more independently minded and shorter blind men, who had walked under and felt the belly, but decided initially on the safe option of agreeing with the group.

"Oh, SHUT UP!" shouted one of the others. "Trust you to always be stirring things up."

The sage spoke. "I see no elephant. I see no palace."

The blind men expostulated in dismay. One of them said, "You see no elephant. You see no palace. Let's find out what you see at the end of my boot." And with that he took a wild swing in the direction of the sage.

"Arrhh! Oooofff!" screamed one of his blind comrades. "Wait till I get my hands on the swine who's just kicked me in the balls!"

Amidst the confusion the sage, and the man who claimed he had seen an elephant, left quietly. Behind them the blind men continued shouting and exchanging blows. A loud trumpeting sound was heard. "Turn it down!" one shouted. "I'm not in the mood for Louis Armstrong!"

A little while later they came to a narrow and dangerous section of the path.

"Tell me, what was it back there?" asked the man, as blind as the fellows they had left behind.

The sage helped the man along the path, but remained silent.

THE BIRTH OF MORTALITY

Papa is carrying my little brother Pierre, and I trot along behind them. We are on a holiday in France, heading for a bridge over a fast-flowing river.

When we are half-way across the bridge we stop to look down at the water. On the left bank there are fishermen with their rods. Pierre, held by Papa, sits on the parapet with legs dangling over the side. Suddenly he gives out a cry; one of his shoes has fallen off and lands in the river with a splash.

A fisherman has seen what's happened and tries to retrieve the shoe with his rod. But he's unsuccessful, and the river carries it away and swallows it up.

We continue to the other side of the bridge and walk through a meadow bursting with colourful flowers. The sun is shining and birds are chirping. Then, to my surprise, darkness suddenly fills my heart like a total eclipse of the sun. During the five years of my existence I've never felt anything like this, or even imagined such a state possible. Such sadness. Am I stuck with this feeling forever?

I want to tell my parents, but how can I explain what is happening? It has to remain my secret. Ten minutes later, as quickly and mysteriously as it had come, the dark mood vanishes. It's as if the sun had turned up its brightness a few notches. Swishing through the tall lush grass, I feel alive.

THE CHALK MOUTH

Arthur Rowbottom didn't enjoy being a school teacher. What he liked best was sleeping.

One Monday morning it was pleasantly warm. "What a fine day for a little nap!" thought Mr Rowbottom. Then he remembered his class.

"What a bother," he muttered to himself. He consulted the textbook. "Open your English books at page 31 and do exercises one to ten. Who made that rude noise? Nigel, was that you again?"

Reluctant pencils moved lazily in response to feeble calls from thirty, listless brains. Mr Rowbottom, hands behind his back, patrolled the aisles with a creaky, plodding gait.

He stopped abruptly next to Kathy. Was she reading comics? Was she writing notes to Kevin Bragg? No, it had nothing to do with Kathy. The unlikely truth was that Arthur Rowbottom had just had an unusually brilliant idea.

He went up to the blackboard and, mumbling inaudibly and concentrating deeply, drew a mouth with a stick of white chalk. Then he sat in his chair, put his feet on the desk, and with a satisfied look on his face soon fell fast asleep.

The reluctant pencils worked slower and slower, until they were going at the speed of a tuckered-out tortoise. Finally, they stopped altogether.

"Get on with your work!" roared Mr Rowbottom. The pencils leapt up with a start and hared down the lines of the exercise books. "I could have sworn he was asleep," whispered Kevin Bragg to his neighbour.

Five minutes later the thirty pencils were slowing down again. "This is the final warning!" roared Mr Rowbottom. "I will not tolerate such behaviour in my classroom!" Again the pencils picked up speed, spewing out the letters of the alphabet like sick donkeys. As for Mr Rowbottom, he slept like a lamb.

Eventually the class understood. It wasn't their teacher speaking to them. It was the mouth on the board. It was impossible, but true – the chalk mouth could talk!

At one point Miss Smart, the deputy head, came in with a message from Mr Ballard, the head. The mouth on the board commanded her to shut up and sit down. Luckily for Mr Rowbottom, at that precise moment he was having a nightmare about a visiting school inspector and woke up. He denied that he had heard anything and called it an auditory hallucination. The children didn't dare contradict him. Poor Miss Smart left wondering if perhaps she had been prescribed the wrong drug.

By the next day the class had got used to the chalk mouth. When it shouted every five minutes, they shouted back. At the end of the afternoon, when Mr Rowbottom examined the exercise books, he discovered that no work had been done. The children had played noughts and crosses and organised races across the top of the desks. On his way home Mr Rowbottom looked thoughtful.

The next morning Mr Rowbottom called out the register and, picking up a fresh piece of chalk, drew a large ear on the board. Anxious whispering filled the room. Mr Rowbottom eased into his favourite position, his eyelids relaxed, and soon he was snoring contentedly.

Well, there was no strident mouth to remind the children what to do, so the class had a marvellous time. But after lunch there was a nasty surprise in store for them. Mr Rowbottom woke up, went over to the board and appeared to be attuning himself to the chalk ear. The ear had heard everything! It had even heard what Kathy had whispered to Kevin Bragg.

That afternoon Mr Rowbottom played among his dreams while the class worked on. The ear on the wall homed in on every scrape and sound. It was better than the NSA.

Thursday came and Mr Rowbottom confidently expected a repeat of yesterday's performance, but when he came to check the exercise books he was dismayed to discover that not a stroke of work had been done. The class had been careful to keep very quiet, but had chosen their own activities. Kathy had written dozens of secret notes to Kevin Bragg, some had played a silent version of battleships, and Nigel Wrigley had composed naughty limericks about Miss Smart.

Friday morning found Mr Rowbottom looking very resolute. He strode up to the blackboard with a box of coloured chalk and drew not a mouth, not an ear, but an eye – a large, red eye.

Seemingly satisfied with his artistic effort, he went back to his desk and settled himself comfortably with the help of a fat pillow he had brought from home. The baleful, red eye watched the class all day. Untiring, it witnessed and recorded every act. At first all the children had stared back at the eye, but one by one they had given up and reluctantly got on with their work.

At break-time, Kevin Bragg went round telling everyone that he had outstared the eye the longest. In actual fact it had been Patrick Smith, who was frightfully thin, but being a shy lad he kept quiet about it.

By the following week the children were getting very miserable, but for Arthur Rowbottom it was bliss. He had almost achieved his life-long ambition of being asleep all the time.

Wednesday was a particularly lovely morning. Mr Rowbottom arrived at school with a deck-chair on the back seat of his car. After touching up the eye on the board and setting the class some more work, he went out and found himself a sunny spot by the games shed.

The thirty pencils were beyond bored that day.

"I think we should fix Rowbottom," cried someone.

"Let's all sign a petition and hand it in to Ballard and Smart," suggested a bright boy.

"They'd never believe us," said Kathy.

"Let's grab all his chalk, so he hasn't got any to draw an eye or anything," suggested Patrick.

"He'd only go and get some more, thicko," said Kevin scornfully.

They fell silent. Nobody had heard Mr Rowbottom coming in. He was furious. "So that's your little game, is it?" he shouted. "Well, we'll soon see about that!"

He marched over to the blackboard and drew another eye, more stern looking than the first one. He drew ears at each corner of the blackboard, and in the middle he drew an enormous mouth. He threw the chalk back into its box, making the dust fly, and without another word headed back to his waiting deck-chair.

Stunned, the children stared at the blackboard. Already the mouth had opened up with a barrage of commands and exhortations. It was going to be such an awful day.

Then, unexpectedly, Patrick Smith stood up and slowly started walking towards the front of the class.

"Sit down, Patrick!" gasped Kathy.

"There's no knowing what that board will do," cried Kevin Bragg, diving under his desk.

Still Patrick continued his slow approach to the blackboard. Ah, but now the eyes had spotted him. The temperature in the classroom seemed to soar as they scorched him with a burning gaze devoid of pity. The ears twitched and stretched as if trying to fly off the blackboard and land on his face to suffocate him. The mouth grew enormous; it screeched and frothed, producing a torrent of sarcastic put-downs.

Now Patrick stood before the ferocious board. The shouting deafened him; the tongue lashed him. The red eyes were grilling him alive, ready for the mouth to swallow the tasty result in one gulp. Some of the children could no longer bear to watch and covered their eyes. Others openly sobbed.

Alone, Patrick stood there. He picked up the duster and with a shaking hand wiped the board clean. The mouth gave out a last, ghostly moan. The eyes popped and then were gone.

The following day there was a new teacher in the classroom, a nice man who liked playing rounders. As for Mr Rowbottom, he was never seen again. It was a complete mystery. It was as if he had been wiped off the face of the Earth.

THE DEAD

So much for, "May he rest in peace". I'm not given a moment to myself; my soul is immediately whisked off to a huge terminal that makes Beijing International Airport look like a service station. Background music is provided by a live harp ensemble. There are sniffer dogs trained to detect hidden sin, though they can be confused if you've recently eaten sausage and bacon. Angelic security guards keep things moving along, and waiting just out of sight there's a scum of Hells Angels in case of riots.

In one corner of this vast space without toilets a confused soul shouts, "But I'm not dead!"

"If you're here it means you're dead," repeats a karma clerk for the third time.

"Look I haven't got time for this," says the soul. "I have a very important meeting to attend. I'm going to be awarded the Nobel Prize in Literature."

The karma clerk checks the notes and makes a sympathetic noise. "Looks like you missed out there, mate. I see your whole life was dedicated to literature and writing, until your heart stopped ticking at age 82. A most worthy winner I'm sure, but you died an hour before the award ceremony."

I reach my designated desk and an efficient-looking karma clerk dressed in blue light has my file ready. But there's a mistake! That's not my name on the cover. I protest. The karma clerk patiently explains that it's not the name I had in my last life; it's my eternal name.

Every second, two more souls arrive without luggage or passport. There is no end in sight.

THE DOLLHOUSE

It's been in our family for years, grand and symmetrical on its table on the landing. This evening some strange urge makes me stoop and look through one of its miniature windows.

I see the dining room with little doll figures sitting at their meal. It is so lovingly detailed that I can almost smell the food.

But this evening something extraordinary is happening: exhibiting exquisite manners, the dolls are bringing forks to the tiny Os of their mouths. The dolls are dining.

A male doll puts down the shred of a napkin and stands. Shocked, I realise that it's dressed exactly the same as me, and its face is a miniature of what greets me in the mirror each morning. I follow the progress of my tiny self up the stairway to a landing and there on a table is a dollhouse.

The doll-me bends down so as to peer through one of its windows. Then it manages to open the window and insert a thumb and forefinger. When these emerge they are gripping a struggling "insect" version of us!

"Hey," I shout to myself, "don't drop me!"

Suddenly, the window behind me rattles loudly and I begin to tremble. I do not turn around because I know that if I do, there – staring at me – will be the biggest EYE I've ever seen.

THE EMPEROR'S NEW CLOTHES

Let's cut to the chase, you know the story. We've reached the part where the emperor is marching in procession before his subjects. A child in the crowd calls out, "The clothes have no emperor!"

At first the child is shushed and told not to talk daft, but then the crowd realises it's true. There's nobody there inside the clothes! Someone shouts, "We have no emperor! Who will rule us and make things happen?"

The child points at the crowd and one by one they realise the same thing is true about them. There are clothes, but nobody is wearing them.

A wise woman croaks, "I've always known this," and there are murmurs of agreement.

That night, when the clothes are piled neatly onto chairs or tossed on the floor, nobody gets into bed, nobody has a bad dream, and nobody is depressed in the morning even though it's Monday.

When the mother of the clear-seeing child opens her front door she sees flowers have been left outside. Puzzled, she notices that some kind of shrine has been erected in his honour. By lunchtime graffiti is appearing on the walls of the town proclaiming that the child is enlightened.

But by evening the realisation has worn off, and once again the clothes ambling around the town are full of mostly fat people.

THE INTENSIFIER

Harold Glebe was about to have his first interesting day. He'd left it rather late. He was seventy, retired, and lonely. The day had started out in the usual manner: empty bladder, fill it up again with tea. Then he had put on his hat, coat and gloves. He had found his stout walking stick in its usual place by the door, and had proceeded down the lane and across the fields.

Harold lived on the edge of a small Devonshire village, a marvellous place for walks. As he entered a small wood, he was startled by a loud shout. "Over here!"

He could not recall a single occasion when anyone had sounded so evidently pleased to see him. He turned in the direction of the voice and was startled to discover a short greenish figure half-hidden behind some bushes. Harold gripped his stick and stood firm.

Satisfied that at least it had the human's attention, the strange being proceeded to tap a small box it was carrying. Then, apparently reading from some kind of display, it said, "Do not be alarmed. Where I come from we all look like this."

Harold was not particularly reassured by this announcement, nor by the next.

"Actually, that's not entirely correct." A bit more tapping produced this explanation: "I beg to inform you that I have accidentally vaporised my legs."

Harold stroked his chin and decided this was probably true. What he had taken to be a dwarfish alien must in fact be an alien minus his legs. Having ascertained the nature of the alien's predicament, he was at a loss as to what to do next. He found himself wondering if perhaps he should have watched more episodes of Star Trek. Would that have helped?

There was also the thought that if something could vaporise the legs off an alien, this thing (whatever it might be) might suddenly go off again and vaporise *his* legs, or even worse.

Plus there was a growing anxiety that he might have to act

167

as a representative of the human race. He was relieved that at least he had put on a clean shirt that morning; but supposing he was asked something tricky like, "And tell us Earthling, what are your beliefs concerning the origin of the universe?"

The answer to that question was always a dead give-away about the relative sophistication of any civilisation. Beliefs that depended upon the improbable antics of elephants and a giant tortoise were bound to be met with discrete titters. If only he had bothered to read that book by Stephen Hawking. He knew it was something to do with a big bang. But how long ago? And what about black holes, where did they fit in? He had a sick feeling he was about to let the side down.

The alien spoke again. "Please help me."

Putting aside his speculations and dropping his stick, Harold responded to this plea. Without further ado he boldly lifted the alien creature.

"I expect you want to be carried back to your spacecraft," he said. "Which way?"

The alien, relieved that he had chanced upon a being with some measure of empathy and intelligence, pointed deeper into the wood. Following the directions indicated by the thin green arm, Harold was eventually guided to a clearing where he saw a dark blue Ford Transit van.

"It's a disguise," said the alien.

The rear doors opened and Harold found himself staring into an interior much larger than the outer spatial dimensions.

"Are you related to the Doctor?" asked Harold.

"Doctor who?" asked the alien.

"Yes," said Harold.

"What?"

At this point Harold's courage deserted him. He stood outside the van shaking. The alien seemed to understand. More tapping on his box.

"Don't panic. It's the ones with the pointy-heads and the big eyes you have to watch out for. Us? We're more interested in inter-galactic parties than boring experiments. Believe me, I have no intention of probing your anal cavity."

The alien gazed at him with inscrutable purple eyes. Harold swallowed and entered cautiously.

Inside the alien vehicle were instrument panels of various kinds, and in the middle a battered-looking, stripy sofa. But the most surprising thing of all was the general air of disorder. Could those possibly be the remains of half-eaten pizzas all over the place?

The alien indicated that he wanted to be placed on a metal tray. As soon as he was securely balanced on this, he was able to float around the cabin with ease. He approached a set of instruments and started pressing buttons.

"What are you doing?" cried Harold in alarm. Was he about to be whisked off across the galaxy to spend the rest of his life cooped up in a glass cage, scratching himself for the amusement of alien offspring?

"Making a cuppa," said the alien. "By the way, now that I'm back home I don't need that portable translation thingy. I kind of see the words I need to speak in my mind."

Harold sat on the sofa and accepted a suspicious-looking drink. Still conscious of his role as Earth representative, he knew it was very important to react correctly to this display of alien hospitality. He decided to use the technique he had employed successfully whilst holding the alien against his own body. Closing his eyes he silently repeated the name *David Attenborough* over and over, like a protective mantra. He swallowed.

"Very good. Very good," said Harold, trying desperately not to retch.

The alien took his drink, gargled with it and then, apparently satisfied, spat it out with gusto.

"Well, thank you for your help," said the alien. "Before you go, it would make me very happy if you would accept a small gift."

Harold noticed that by the alien's side there was a container full of various objects: beads, baubles, mirrors, and some other objects he could not identify. The alien selected what looked like a watch and attached it to Harold's left wrist.

"Goodbye."

"Uh, goodbye," said Harold.

Having got this far and survived, he realised that actually he felt reluctant to leave. It was not every day he had a chance to communicate with someone.

"Going far?" he ventured.

"No, just a hop. If I leave now I should avoid the rush hour on Alpha Centauri. But you never know these days, there's bound to be space lane closures all over the bloody place."

After a brief chat about the rising price of energy, the earthling was finally shooed out. The Transit van did a three-point turn, rose into the sky, and disappeared above the clouds. All that remained was a slight depression in the ground and what looked like oil stains.

"Extraordinary!" thought Harold as he walked back home. Already he was beginning to see the incident as something in the past, something to add to his memoirs. But in fact his adventure was only just beginning.

Having made himself a good strong cup of proper tea, Harold sat at home and examined the alien watch carefully. It was black and tough-looking. The strap was made of interlocking metal links. Disappointed, he noticed that it only had one hand, which was set to the twelve o'clock position. On the right-hand half of the face there were a number of regular gradations. He counted ten. On the left-hand side there was nothing, except for a strange hieroglyph at the nine o'clock position. He held the watch to his ear, but it made no sound. However, he had the peculiar impression of some kind of faint, throbbing sensation going up his arm.

He turned the winder, and the hand moved smoothly to the first position. At the same instant a shaft of sunlight burst in through the window and lit up the room. The Beethoven symphony that had been playing quietly on the radio suddenly produced some loud blasts. And a bitter taste of tea stung the inside of his mouth. Slightly alarmed, he stood up and walked towards the radio. On the way he caught his knee on a low table, and rolled about on the floor in agony. What had he done to his knee? Why were the birds singing so loudly? And why did the carpet feel so strange?

The intricate folds of his trousers caught his attention. He found he could not take his eyes off them. In that still moment there was a glimmer of understanding. He carefully turned the hand on the watch back to its initial position. Immediately the colours in the room faded slightly, the sounds from the birds and the radio became attenuated, and the pain subsided.

He relaxed for a moment, and then moved the hand to position three. Once again the folds of his trousers caught his attention. He seemed to be floating above a wonderful landscape of valleys and hills. His eyes took in every twisting feature of the polyester and wool surface. He had once toured Scotland, but nothing he had seen there could compare with the beauty of this.

His attention was distracted by a change in the sound coming from the radio. The music had stopped and a voice began relating the day's events. As usual it was fairly awful, but for poor Harold, with his super-sensitivity, it was horrific. He listened aghast at the state of his world. When it was over there was music and Harold was weeping. But at least one good thing had come out of it. All his life he had found it difficult to know what to do; he had never been sure about anything (and he wasn't even certain about that). How he envied people with confidence, ambition and career plans. It had taken seventy years, but at long last the pale, scratchy lines on the blueprint of his life were beginning to form some kind of meaningful pattern. His mission was clear: he must kill himself now to avoid any further pointless suffering.

But how? That was the question. He was damned if he was going to slash his wrists and make his final gesture on earth one that involved so much mess. Gassing was out too (no mains gas in the village) and he didn't own a car. He considered an overdose of painkillers. Yes, that would do very nicely. If you swallowed enough, it cured the pain by removing the experiencer of the pain. But then he remembered there were no painkillers in the cottage. He didn't really need them because he never suffered from headaches. So that was the reason for this apparent blessing! It was just so that some vindictive god, with a warped sense of humour, could gloat over him at this precise moment of his life. It had all been leading up to this!

However, he did keep a good length of rope under the stairs. Changing his plan and shielding his eyes from the vivid colours he had never noticed before, he found the rope and made his way into the garden. The breeze outside felt like a gale. The photons from the sun played rapid ping-pong on his bare skin. Green grass, green grass, GREEN, GREEN, GREEN, went his brain as he crossed the lawn. He tried to keep his eyes fixed on the big apple tree at the bottom of the garden. Its branches waved and its leaves shook like tambourines, encouraging him on his way. He walked slowly, carefully putting one foot in front of the other, while all around the playful spirits of nature plucked at his senses, and made all his nerve endings jump and shriek.

He reached the tree and threw the rope. It went over a convenient branch first time. As he went to retrieve the dangling end, he happened to catch sight of a flower. It was a common daisy, but to Harold it was the most beautiful thing he had ever seen. He genuflected before the daisy in awe.

Finding one end of the rope still in his hand, he laughed and stood up to remove it from the tree. Unfortunately, the manoeuvre caused him to lose his footing and flatten the miraculous daisy. This monstrous act shook him out of his mind-expanded state. He quickly wound the watch hand back to the noon position, ending any further agony or ecstasy that day.

Over the next few days Harold savoured more pleasure than he had experienced in the entirety of his previous life. He had learnt his lesson the first day. He tried to be careful not to have the intensifier (as he now called the "watch") switched on when anything potentially unpleasant might happen. But of course that was difficult to predict. He knew what it felt like to go from the heaven of enjoying fish and chips to the hellish pain of accidentally biting your tongue at intensity three.

The highest intensity he had dared was five, while eating

creamed rice pudding and tinned peaches (a favourite since childhood). It had resulted in celestial bliss, but he was aware of the dangers. It wasn't just that an unexpected piece of peach stone might hurt his tooth. It was also that if someone had come in at that moment and suggested he sell his soul for a bowl of rice pudding, Harold would have found it quite impossible to resist.

He pondered on the matter of his unexpected good fortune in receiving such a special gift. It was almost certainly the result of a muddle. The green alien had no doubt wanted to give the "native" a cheap watch, but somehow quite a different sort of gadget had ended up in the gift box. He recalled the untidiness of the alien craft.

Of course sometimes he wondered what it would be like to set the intensifier to position ten, and he puzzled over the meaning of the mysterious symbol at nine o'clock. There was also the question of what to do should the alien return to reclaim his device. Harold took no special precautions; he merely continued to lock the doors carefully last thing at night, as he had done all his life.

After a few days of experimenting and reflecting, he woke up one morning with the powerful conviction that there had to be more to life than tinned rice pudding. He possessed a most amazing contraption, something that could amplify sensations and emotions, but what did he have to amplify? Nothing but a grey, empty life. Take Harold Glebe and multiply him by a million, you still ended up with practically nothing.

There was something else. He did not want the world to know about the intensifier (he could not imagine anything worse than having his life turned upside-down by the media, or by prying government agents) but at the same time he longed to share his good fortune. What fun it would be to introduce someone else to the intensifier. Let's face it, what Harold needed was a woman. However there was a problem. By no stretch of the imagination could Harold be described as a man of the world. Even "man of the village" was an exagerration – "ghost of the village" was more like it. Apart from buying groceries, his main interaction with village life consisted of going down to the *Rat and Parrot* once a week. There, he would have a brief exchange with the landlord; after which he would choose the quietest-looking corner and nurse his pint until it would have looked odd if he stayed any longer.

Harold had no idea where he was going to find a woman to share his secret. But for once luck was on his side: a few days later, while in the gents of the *Rat and Parrot*, he overheard a conversation between two men. They were talking about someone called Janice, who worked the till in the garage just outside the village. He learnt some astounding facts about her anatomy. Somehow he knew she was the one.

The night after the pub incident Harold had a strange dream. He was sitting on a sunny beach. Out of the sea appeared a dark blue Ford Transit van. It drove across the top of the waves towards him. At the wheel was a wonderful woman with long golden curls. She seemed to be smiling and winking at him. The van pulled up on the sand and she approached him, wearing a short thin skirt and a shirt tied at the waist.

"Hi, I'm Janice. What's your name?" she breathed.

"Harry," croaked Harold.

Nobody had ever called him Harry, but it suited the new persona the dream had conjured up. Janice now stood very close to him and took his hand. Before Harry could react, the rear doors of the van burst open. The green alien with the purple eyes floated up on his tray.

"I believe these are mine," he said sternly.

There was a flash and a sensation of intense heat. Harry found himself without legs. For a brief moment he remained suspended in mid-air, then his body crashed down and the stumps buried themselves in the sand. Janice and the alien returned to the van, which vanished back into the sea. Harry too was gone. Harold was back watching the sea, which seemed to be getting closer by the minute. He could do nothing as the waves began to tease him and retreat, and then to pound him with hearty slaps. Before long his lungs began to fill...

Harold woke up before he drowned, not at all discouraged by the dream. He washed and dressed more carefully than usual. In his bedroom he pulled back a section of the carpet. He then loosened a floorboard and felt for something. His hand reappeared holding a metal box and inside it were thick wads of notes. Alas, poor Harold believed that money was the only thing he had to offer. He stuffed notes into his purse and replaced the box.

What followed was intensely painful and stressful for Harold and involved many sudden retreats, but finally he concluded his transaction with Janice in the garage outside the village. She wasn't like the Janice in his dream. She was a middle-aged woman with short hair and a puffy face. He was astonished to hear his own voice introduce himself as Harry and actually speak the words he had rehearsed, but in the end it all happened quite smoothly, given that each could provide what the other wanted. The arrangement was that Janice would come to his cottage that Sunday.

The rest of the week Harold did not even think of using the intensifier. Without the gadget all his senses seemed extraordinarily acute. He kept seeing things he had never noticed before. For example, he discovered he had hair growing out of his ears. How could he use a mirror every day and never have seen that?

The day of the assignation he changed the sheets, washed his hair, found some after-shave, and of course trimmed his ears. He went to the wood and picked wild flowers. He arranged them in a vase on top of the chest in his bedroom. Then he removed the flowers and threw them on the compost heap. Minutes later he changed his mind and retrieved the flowers. He couldn't eat anything.

Janice arrived. She took off her raincoat and inspected the cottage.

"Would you like a drink?"

"No, thanks," she said.

I expect she just wants to get it over with, thought Harold sadly. They entered the bedroom and Janice noticed the flowers.

"They're nice."

Next to the flowers Harold had placed a bundle of notes. He knew he had left too much, but he didn't care. She began to undress slowly, all the while keeping her eyes on the flowers (or possibly the money). Harold's trembling hand was poised over the intensifier. At last she removed her bra and pants, and moved across to the bed. He took in the full titanic majesty of her wobbling buttocks at intensity three.

Janice lay under the quilt and closed her eyes. Harold, whose usual bedtime companion was a cocoa mug, undressed with enormous difficulty. His hands were shaking, and it felt like ants were crawling all over his fingers. He was overloaded with messages from everywhere and everything. Finally, he got into bed and pushed against her.

"You don't need cranking, do you luv?" she laughed. Then she noticed the big black watch. "Oi, you planning to time me?"

Harold said nothing. He couldn't. Just before getting into bed he had moved the intensifier on to position five. As he held Janice he had the impression that he could feel the individual molecules of her body penetrating his skin. Her molecules were hot, and their electrons played a tantalising game of quantum hide-and-seek. He could see her, or he could feel her, but it was impossible to do both at the same time. It was too much. He moved away and lay on his back. Janice took this to be an indication of his favourite position. Expertly she mounted him and took him inside her AND THEY'RE OFF!

It was like a horse race: it was like winning the Grand National and being trampled to death at the same time. It was like a space mission: one moment soaring up into space, and the next crashing down into the stormy Atlantic. Occasionally he managed to open his eyes. He saw wild breasts hopping around like kangaroos in a bush fire. He saw her face. Once all the features seemed rubbery and grotesquely magnified, then he looked again and she was as bewitching as the wispy Orion Nebula.

"Am I hurting you, Harry?" she asked.

"Don't stop," he begged.

Finally, it did stop. It ended with the most intensely pleasurable orgasm in the history of human orgasms. Of all the most unlikely people on Earth it was Harold Glebe who could claim this honour.

Totally spent, Harold lay unmoving and was so far away he had no awareness of Janice's growing alarm. She slapped his face, but he felt nothing.

"Holy mother of God, he's croaked it!"

Harry had died on her, or rather under her. She dressed quickly, grabbed the money, and fled surreptitiously from the cottage.

When Harold regained a semblance of normal consciousness he did a rather foolish thing. The main trouble with good experiences is that they come to an end. The usual reaction is to wish to repeat them. For example, have another drink, except maybe this time to make it a double. Harold immediately turned the intensifier up to position ten. It was only then that he realised the bed was empty. This was followed by a deafening, crashing noise, which was the sound of his voice calling for Janice. There was no answer. He propped himself up, and noticed that the flowers looked enormous and were singing. Then he saw with horror that the bed was crawling with thousands of bugs! He jumped out and hopped up and down, finding the sensation of the carpet on his naked feet unbearable. His tried to turn back the hand on the intensifier, but it wouldn't budge. It was stuck at position ten. Ignoring the choir of flowers, and the carnivorous carpet eating his feet, he decided to take off the watch. His fingers fumbled at the strap, but the metal links seemed fused together. He tried to wrench it off and screamed.

When Harold came round, he remembered what had happened. Some of the hairs on his arm were trapped in the strap. The amplified pain had caused him to faint. Once more he tried and failed to turn back the winder, or to slide off the intensifier. Desperate, he paused and listened to the eerie percussive background song of the cottage. The colours and pattern of what had once seemed like faded wallpaper burned into his eyes and made them water. His nose, too, itched and dripped. He managed to open the top drawer of the chest and fumbled about for a pair of sunglasses. Then he stuffed tissues in his ears and up his nose. Anything to dull his senses.

Naked except for the sunglasses, and with bits of tissue sticking out of him, Harold lurched towards the top of the stairs. Even walking was tricky, because of the transmogrification of the cottage into something surreal and alive. Like a child he descended the stairs backwards on his hands and knees, while sudden loud creaks ricocheted all around him. Every few seconds he had to rest to prevent his brain and eyeballs from bursting.

Eventually he reached the backdoor and, still on his hands and knees, crawled across the lawn towards the garden bench. Sitting on the bench he waited for a dark blue Transit van. His only hope now was for the alien to save him, just as once he had saved the alien.

Harold felt the tremor of earthworms burrowing in the ground beneath his feet. He actually saw that *every* single blade of grass was slowly growing. He heard the sound of military marching, coming from a column of ants.

He closed his eyes and became aware that millions of creatures silently went about their business inside the hidden and bountiful world of his body. Some were ensconced in convenient nooks and crannies, and lived sedentary lives; while others were more adventurous, and rode the currents and rapids of his pulsating fluids.

And there was the constant movement of thought. He was able to follow the trains, synapse by synapse, across the immense marshalling yard of his mind. It did not seem to him that the human brain was intelligent at all. It was all very simple, just repetitive patterns; a flow of chemical electricity going down well-worn channels, most of them laid down before he was born.

He opened his eyes and saw the sky. He did not see its colour, or its expanse, or the shape of the individual clouds. He saw the totality and it seemed that in that perception there was no observer. For a timeless moment there was only THIS – an intense real beauty beyond description.

When "Harold" returned he saw the erotic pink of the

sunset change slowly to blood red, and then become a slow descent towards the blackness of death.

For the last time he adjusted the intensifier. Just as he had anticipated, the hand would not go back, but it would go forwards. The instant it reached the mysterious symbol, beyond the end of the measurable scale, the garden disappeared. There was a bitter taste of metal in his mouth, then an impression of matter being created out of enormous energies. Across his consciousness flashed scenes of deserts, ice-fields, jungles and cities. He felt he was swimming, crawling, flying and walking – all at the same time. He felt the pain of multiple births and deaths simultaneously. He starved while gorging on rich food. He entered a million orifices, and was entered a million times. He was murdered and he killed, he swore and he prayed. He was even a dark blue Transit van hovering high above the village. He was a green alien with purple eyes. He was the thought inside an alien brain, "Too late."

EVERYTHING collapsed to a singularity. Immediately Harold's hair burst into flames, and a fierce light shot from his head into the sky like reverse lightning. Black balloons of smoke drifted upwards as his body began to melt. Within a surprisingly short time it was reduced to a bubbling substance that flowed off the bench, and finally cooled into a pile of dust on the grass. The intensifier remained on the bench. That night it was collected.

A few days later the local news-sheet reported that one of the residents of the village had totally combusted after being struck by lightning. In the *Rat and Parrot,* folk offered up their own theories, and commented wryly on the mysterious goings-on in the universe. There was also a report of a UFO sighting. The witness complained that it was stupid to call it a UFO, when it was such a familiar object that one could find on any road.

***

The priest waited impatiently until he was quite certain nobody was coming. The rain had stopped and the cemetery was mostly still, except for an occasional drip. The physical remains of Harold Glebe were buried among the yew trees; the last step of his journey from dust to dust had been carried out most efficiently. The priest trudged back to the church and mounted his bicycle. As he cycled home the rain started up again and fell on his glasses, preventing him from seeing the stunning beauty that lay all around.

THE SCISSORS OF THE EGO

One night in August 1990 I went for a moonlit walk in a deserted part of the New Forest. An image came to me of a man cutting himself out of the background of life with the scissors of the ego. Now he thinks that, unlike the trees, he is free to wander and do what he likes. But instead of freedom and happiness, he finds fear and a terrible sense of loneliness. Finally, after many years, he is forced to become still, and he sees in the background of life a hole shaped just like him. His arms, legs and head fit the gap perfectly. As he breathes in, the air snaps into his lungs like the last piece of a jigsaw puzzle. Reconnected to everything, the dividing lines across the world vanish.

THE SECRET

Maud strode across the room and flung open the window. "Piss!" she cried. "That's all it ever smells of in here – piss!"

Her sister Penny, sitting on the sofa, made no response. The nine cats taking up every spare inch of the sofa looked on disdainfully.

Maud headed back to the door, but on the way her short, stout figure fell over a pile of books.

"I correct myself," she said acidly, getting back to her feet. "Piss and mouldy old books, that's all it ever smells of in here." Penny, a retired librarian, had not lost her love of books. There were books everywhere. Books and cats were her passion. "Well," she said, "at least you should be glad it's only nine cats now."

Maud laughed grimly. "Only nine! Yes indeed, how grateful I am that you finally had the good sense to rid us of some of them. It was getting quite ridiculous, and you know we couldn't afford to feed them. One can only hope that such a fit of reason won't be as rare as a hot summer."

Penny gave a secret wink to her favourite cat, a Siamese called Esmeralda.

"Ah, there you are Penny," said Maud. "I was looking for you. Where have you been?"

"In the garden."

"In the garden! What, in this weather? What were you doing in the garden?"

"Weeding."

"Weeding! At this time of the year? Have you gone quite mad?"

Avoiding Maud's gaze, Penny inserted herself amongst her beloved cats on the sofa.

"I hope you remembered to lock the shed," Maud grumbled. "If you ask me there's something fishy going on around here, and I'm not referring to the cats' expensive supper!"

Maud navigated the hillocks of books and disappeared into the vestibule, to look for her wellies. "I'm going to get to the bottom of this," she called out.

Alone with her cats Penny tried to cuddle Esmeralda, but the Siamese pulled away as if wanting to put as much distance as possible between herself and Penny. Her animal instincts had detected an impending storm.

They both stiffened as they heard a distant scream of annoyance. Maud had discovered the secret at the bottom of the garden.

THE TABLECLOTH

Disciple: Tea, Master?

Master: Thank you. Oh, what a lovely tablecloth! These coloured circles represent the different individual egos, but look at the one background: the tablecloth. That is the undifferentiated Reality, the All.

Disciple: But Master, this tablecloth has been cut from a bigger piece!

Master: Ah, all grand-sounding, supposedly all-encompassing theories are limited! I bow before your wisdom.

THIS DRUG IS TOO GOOD

I won't bore you with the long chemical name, or how it interacts with neurotransmitters. Suffice it to say this drug is good – and bad. Millions have died using it, but that doesn't seem to have slowed down its spread.

The main effect is an absolutely potent hallucination billions of light years across. You can see objects, hear them, smell them, taste them, and even feel them. There are wonderful highs; however, some report really bad trips. At the moment it's legal, but I don't know how long that will last.

What's amazing is that no lab tests were done, yet somehow everyone started using it. Even a small dose and you are transported to a place of vivid colours, exotic sounds, and "endless forms most wonderful". I would like to give it up and go back to just being, but this drug is too good.

THE WAREHOUSE

There are many words that mean big. Choose any, such as gigantic, immense, monstrous... or stack them all up. It doesn't make any difference. Nothing can rightly convey the size of the warehouse. I've been working here since I was a child. I have no memories of any previous life, and don't recall the face of my parents. Early on I realised it made sense to stay here rather than go home, so I found an empty room where I could stay.

There are so many long corridors and rooms here. If I asked you to count them it would kill you. I expect in your culture the largest number that has been given a specific name is a googolplex. That doesn't even begin to cover it. Yes, yes, I know there's infinity, but I don't like to go there. How could I possibly do my job if the number of rooms was infinite? It gives me a headache just to think about it. Yet somehow it all gets done, and my conscientiousness has never been questioned.

In this warehouse are stored all possibilities: every single possible event. This is where they are stacked up, waiting and ready to go. My job is to take the next one down to the launch bay of Reality, and press the actualisation button. It never ends, however I manage to keep on top. I may talk slowly, but I work fast.

In fact I've given myself the nickname "the busy one," although sometimes for a change I refer to myself as Gottfried. But I don't mind, because it means there is no time to worry about anything. Also I realise I have the easy job. All I do is wheel the possibilities down to the bay and press the button. My Boss has the hard job. She has to work out which is the next best possibility. But it's amazing, she always gets it right.

I've learnt not to ask too many questions. Once I was having a bad day and it all seemed futile. So I asked the Boss, "All the ready-made possibilities not being currently realised are happy to sit quietly in their rooms. They seem totally indifferent to whether they get picked to go down to the launch bay. And in a way I get it. When I press the button and give them existence, isn't it just a pseudo-actuality, given they're already here in this warehouse?" The boss refused to answer.

Another time I said to her, "Instead of choosing the next best possibility, why not launch all of them simultaneously?" She got really angry and gave me a right telling-off!

So that's it, that's my life, except I also have to sweep the floor and keep an eye out for time rats. Their whiskers are so sensitive they can detect even a single chronon.

Next possible event being actualised NOW!

THE MYSTERY OF MARSHAM

The grave was small, and when I say small I mean mouse-sized. The name on the plain headstone said "Harold Glebe". It was highly unlikely that a child would call her pet mouse "Harold Glebe" and her parents arrange for a burial in an official cemetery.

Having finished my tour of the church I walked back to the village of Marsham and entered the pub. It was empty except for two old codgers sitting in a corner. Having settled on a pint of the local brew I asked the barmaid if she knew anything about the grave of Harold Glebe. One of the old timers sputtered into his beer and the barmaid turned pale.

"I don't talk about it," she said with a Westcountry accent. "I'm betwaddled enough as it is just dealing with me customers."

I felt my presence was unwanted, so put down my beer mug and walked out. Back in the car I found I could get a bit of a signal so googled, "Harold Glebe Marsham". This is what I read:

It did not require many pall bearers to carry Harold Glebe to his final resting place. His entire remains fitted inside a matchbox. What caused his death remains a profound mystery. The original supposition that he had been struck by lightning has been discounted by weather experts.

At the inquest held yesterday at the Coroner's Offices for Torbay and South Devon, extracts were read out from Mr Glebe's diary. They recount how, on one of his walks, he had chanced upon a stricken alien and helped him back to his space vehicle. The alien, grateful for the help, had presented Mr Glebe with a gift.

Given the unusual nature of the case, and the fact there was no other plausible explanation, the coroner pronounced a verdict of death by misadventure caused by the misuse of advanced alien technology. The police report states that no alien artefact was recovered at the scene of death.

UNIVERSE 109

Dr Amy Reynolds walked briskly down the long corridor. She was one of those people who it's disconcerting to greet. Some days she would smile at you, but other times she would walk straight past. It was more a matter of preoccupation with the burdens of her job than of unkindness. She walked past Tom Dickens, the director, without even glancing at him, but this was precisely because she had seen him.

Now she stopped outside a white door, and peered in through the glass panel. She glanced down at her bundle of notes. What relevance did they have to James, the young man inside? Hospitalised nearly all his life, and totally withdrawn from the world of others, he was now engaged in an animated conversation with Nurse Jenkins. It was as if a new personality had miraculously surfaced in the body once occupied by poor James. The "birth" had not been without its traumas. The patient, who had never been known to leave his room voluntarily, had stormed out shouting, "At last, I remember!" Once the storm had receded (with the aid of injections), a remarkable treasure had been left washed up on the beach.

Dr Reynolds opened the door with some degree of apprehension. Any joy she might have felt, as a result of this professional success, was marred by its total unexpectedness. Nurse Jenkins turned to look at her and seemed to hesitate. She dismissed him with a wave of her hand and approached the patient with a smile.

"Good morning, James."

"Good morning, doctor. You may still call me James if you wish, but I think you should know that it is not my real name."

Dr Reynolds was so surprised that she couldn't speak. It was not what she had heard that had startled her, but the look of extraordinary alertness and intelligence that met her gaze. She glanced down at her notes for a second time, and was reminded of the report that the patient had spent several hours the previous day exploring every square inch of his room with every sense at his disposal, even to the extent of licking and apparently tasting the surfaces.

When she looked up she saw that he had lowered his head, his dark hair falling forwards.

"I was not myself before," he said in a quiet voice. "It's only these past few days that I have remembered who I really am. I don't quite know how to put this. There is no easy way to make you understand..." He looked up at her, and she felt the look was originating from some shimmering, far-off place.

Dr Reynolds waited, and then said, "You are about to tell me who you really are."

"Yes. I am the Lord, the God of all this universe."

Dr Reynolds had witnessed many bizarre things in the course of her professional life and she merely resigned herself to the fact there had been no miracle cure.

James lifted up his hands as if to impart a blessing, "There is no need to worship me or anything daft like that. I would much rather we carried on as before. Doctor! You're leaving? I do enjoy talking with you. Humans are quite fascinating from this angle."

"I'll see you this afternoon, James."

There was an expression of joy on James' face. "Doctor?"

"Yes?"

"Could you take your clothes off, please?"

Dr Reynolds stared at him for a moment and left without seeking an explanation.

James, now alone, let his gaze wander about the sparse room with its light green walls. He noticed some biscuits left by nurse Jenkins. He undid the packet of Hobnobs and nibbled one experimentally. "So, this is eating a biscuit," he said to himself, giving all his attention to the pleasant taste and crumbly texture.

As he relaxed, his mind seemed to slip its present anchor. The feel of his human body became a warm fuzzy ball of dull sensation. Then, suddenly, it was gone, and he luxuriated in the relative freedom of his true form – a vibrating pattern of energy.

It existed within the matrix of energies that constituted the Orf universe. As Guardian and seed of Universe 109 it was his duty to report to the Orf Total Consciousness.

The Guardian hopped from one side of the universe to the other. He found it relaxing, and it helped his thinking. Pausing, he shared the same physical location as ten to the power of fifty busy karma clerks.

The reports had started soon after the greatest event in Orf history, when a premature "Big Crunch" had been engineered. As the universe had accelerated towards a singularity and the final moment of history, the energy generated had been used to pull back a nonillionth of a second before the end of time. The total involution of space-time had stalled at a point where it was possible for the Orf Total Consciousness to reach momentary absolute unity, and to pull back to a kind of universal Bodhisattva state. This event had been eagerly anticipated for thousands of years. The great plan was to ask the important question never before satisfactorily answered: Does God exist? The question having been asked, the answer had come.

"I DO NOT KNOW."

The OTC had absorbed its colossal disappointment before enquiring of itself how it could find out. The OTC had answered itself immediately.

"USING THE COMPLETE POWER AND TOTAL KNOWLEDGE FINALLY AVAILABLE TO ME SINCE THE INTEGRATION OF THE UNIVERSE, I HAVE TRIED EVERY PERMUTATION AND EXPLORED ALL LOGICAL AVENUES. THE ONLY WAY THE QUESTION COULD POSSIBLY BE ANSWERED IS BY INTRODUCING A NEW 'X' FACTOR. SINCE I AM EVERYTHING, THERE IS ABSOLUTELY NOWHERE THIS CAN BE FOUND. THE ONLY WAY IS TO ABANDON ORDER AND TO PLUNGE INTO CHAOS. IN RANDOMNESS LIES THE ONLY POSSIBILITY OF SUCCESS."

After this brief but shattering encounter with itself, the individual Orf minds had seeded out from the ocean-oneness of the Orf

Total Consciousness and the extremely dense, but intricately complex, universe had stabilised at its current dimensions of approximately a single hydrogen atom. To the re-incarnated Orfs the OTC remained as a subtle background presence: a Holistic Ghost.

The rule-loving, logical Orfs had been faced with the unthinkable. Embrace chaos? Never! However, they had developed a cunning plan that left the orderly, miniaturised Orf universe unthreatened. The Orfs had created virtual sub-universes. Trillions of them. Each one was a carefully monitored experiment in balance between order and chaos. Each had a Guardian. But all had a subsidiary existence. They were like dreams dreamt by a dreamer: a real dream, a real dreamer, but a dream nevertheless.

Within the field of his consciousness the Guardian had formed a tiny seed which, through the application of simple rules together with the immense power of recursion, had eventually become a playground for galaxies, stars and myriad beings, a vast space-time arena, where countless possibilities emerged, fought, cooperated, flourished or died.

Then he waited. Waited for what? He did not know. If he had known, there would have been no point to it all. The great Orf experiment had in its underpinning equation the term "hope," hope that the missing ingredient necessary for solving the metaphysical riddle would (if encountered) be recognisable.

So the master engineer of the subtle interplay between laws and randomness nursed the controls of the universe, adding a little chaos when it became too static and a little harmony when its creative play edged towards total destruction.

Nurse Jenkins sat back and rested his feet on the wooden table in the patient's room. He was about the same age and height as James, but much stockier. Although he had worked as a nurse for about three years, he did not consider it his career. His real ambition was to make a living as a writer.

"Have a biscuit, God," he said pushing over the packet he had left the previous day.

"No, thank you, Alan. I have already tried that. You may take them with you when you leave."

"Go on, have one," insisted Jenkins.

"You don't understand," explained James. "There are many experiences I wish to sample during my time on Earth. But why bother to repeat them?"

Jenkins shrugged and glanced at the door to make sure nobody was about to come in. Suppressing an evil grin, he said, "If you're really God, as you claim, then make this table vanish right now!"

James looked shocked. "Why? What's wrong with it?"

"Nothing's wrong with it, but how are people expected to believe you're God if you don't perform the odd miracle?"

"What they believe about me," said James, "makes no difference one way or the other."

"Funny God you are," snorted Jenkins, helping himself to a biscuit and dropping crumbs everywhere. "I thought the whole idea of Gods incarnating was to set the world aright, but all you seem to want to do is a spot of sightseeing!"

"Alan, I'm not here to make radical changes. It's taken long enough just to remember who I really am. I hadn't anticipated that taking on this illusory, human form would be so debilitating. I might start a chain-reaction of errors if I attempted to meddle with the universe in my present befuddled state. No, I'm afraid the universe must continue to coast for a while."

"I see," mused Jenkins, looking at James intently. Everyone in the institution was talking about him. He was certainly more stimulating to be with than no end of supposedly sane people he knew. In fact Jenkins always left feeling strangely refreshed and invigorated. "And how long do you intend to stay down here?"

"Until I've completed my investigation. I want to know what it feels like to be a limited being. What is it like to operate across such narrow bandwidths? But do you know, it's a lot more interesting than I had ever imagined. I looked at the sunrise this morning..."

He stopped, as if lost in admiration for his colourful handiwork. "Actually, I thought I might pick up some clue."

"Clue?"

"Oh, it's too complicated to explain." James looked troubled and preoccupied.

"What about me?" asked Jenkins. "What's going to happen when I die?"

"That depends on the calculations of the karma clerks. We have to maximise the potential for rapid evolution." James suddenly brightened. "I like you, Alan. I know you come to see me sometimes during your breaks. Perhaps when I'm back *home* some subtle tweaking of the cosmos might be in order. Tell me, how would you like to spend the rest of your life?"

"Why, God, that's really kind of you to fix it for me." Jenkins settled back in his chair and closed his eyes. "I see myself living in a disused lighthouse. The majestic view inspires me. It seems I have several best-selling books under my belt. Now I see a beautiful woman —"

His reverie was interrupted by James. "That reminds me."

"Oh, the magazines! Sorry, I forgot," apologised Jenkins. "I'll bring them tomorrow."

"Obviously as Designer in Chief it's not that I'm unfamiliar with the female form," explained the patient. "It's just that I'm curious to test the effect through human eyes."

"Sure thing!" winked Jenkins.

They both looked at the door.

"I have to get out soon," said James. "There's a long list of experiences I'd like to tick off."

As Jenkins left he felt a pang of guilt. The reason he had been visiting the patient outside his duty roster was because it was inspiring his latest story. But he was beginning to feel for James.

The Guardian listened to the electromagnetic murmurings of the busy karma clerks. Some worked for him, plotting the deeds of the consciousness-units in Universe 109. Physical bodies were constantly being destroyed, but consciousness-units were a different matter. After all, they were all sparks from the fire of his own dear self. The precious units were recycled again and again to animate the many forms that lived out lives shaped by the calculations of the karma clerks.

The Guardian meditated and attuned himself to the ghostly presence of the Orf Total Consciousness. He felt the exquisitely beautiful pattern of energy that danced majestically at his centre.

"CREATOR AND GUARDIAN OF UNIVERSE 109, I AWAIT YOUR REPORT."

"O Holistic Ghost, of all the worlds in my universe, one excites my frequencies more than any other."

"SPEAK OF IT."

"It is a small world, one of eight main planets, orbiting an average star. It is the home of three creatures that have captured my interest."

"WHY THIS INTEREST?"

"I suspect they may have discovered the Truth-beyond-our-knowledge."

"WHY DO YOU SUSPECT THIS?"

"The karma clerks can find no trace of these creatures. It is as if they had vanished from the total scheme of things. That's impossible from the standpoint of our science. Either they have attained some new state of freedom, as yet unimagined by us, or else there is an error in the Reincarnation Database. However, as we know, the karma clerks have been programmed for infallibility."

"DO THE CREATURES SPEAK OF THE TRUTH-BEYOND-OUR-KNOWLEDGE?"

"Possibly, but each speaks of it in a different way. One expressed the paradoxical view that you must love your enemies."

"I HAVE NO ENEMIES. AGGRESSION HAS CEASED TO EXIST. THEREFORE, THIS METHOD IS INAPPLICABLE."

"He also said that we must become like little children."

"I CANNOT REGRESS, I AM LOGICALLY PERFECT, BUT THE SUB-UNIVERSES ARE LIKE CHILDREN. THROUGH THEIR PLAY THIS ADVICE IS FOLLOWED. THE OUTCOME IS AWAITED."

The Guardian continued, "Another said we must follow the middle way through life."

"I CANNOT FOLLOW ANY PATH BUT THE ONE I AM ON. IT IS THE MOST LOGICALLY PERFECT, ACCOMMODATING ALL KNOWN FACTS, BACKED BY A MASSIVELY PARALLEL FAULT-TOLERANT SYSTEM. THERE IS NO OTHER PATH. CALL MINE THE MIDDLE WAY IF YOU MUST."

"The third creature taught that the mind itself is the cause of ignorance. One must stop all thought. Awareness must be perfectly still and empty; then the Truth-beyond-our-knowledge will take care of the rest."

"STOP ALL THOUGHT! I AM PURE THOUGHT. IF I STOP THINKING, I AM NO MORE. WHERE THEN IS TRUTH?"

The Guardian was silent. He wondered whether to add that the second creature had indeed spoken of a supreme emptiness, but decided against it.

"GO NOW AND WATCH YOUR WORLDS."

It was over until the next time. The Guardian began hopping from one side of the universe to the other. But instead of relaxing him, it brought a strange feeling he could not identify, because it was almost totally alien to him. Was it fear? Fear had come from somewhere, or from deep within. Of course the universe was poised near its final moment, but Orf power held it safely in stasis. They had the entire energy of the universe at their disposal. But what was on the other side of the final event, when the last nonillionth of a second popped away? Surely the Orf Total Consciousness was real and would remain? Surely in that infinitesimal instant *everything* could not possibly become *nothing*? The Guardian shuddered, producing disturbing diffraction patterns. Then he remembered his duty, and with customary diligence returned to observing his epic dream.

Jenkins sat alone in a quiet corner of the canteen, empty plate pushed to one side, biro poised. "Damn!" he muttered. The story had been going so well, but now he was completely bogged down. He groaned and rubbed his face vigorously. Perhaps it would help if he knew the ending. His stories had a habit of suddenly appearing out of nowhere and growing profusely in all directions like bindweed. The biro began to prune words, lines and even entire paragraphs, altering the destiny of the main protagonist, who was simply called "JT". Thoroughly dissatisfied, he closed the exercise book, stuffed it in his pocket, and returned to his duties.

Not long afterwards he entered James's room and found it empty. He could imagine a number of plausible reasons for this, but there arose a suffocating feeling of anxiety. He walked across to the window, which looked out over the drive leading up to the institution. He was astonished to see about a dozen people down below, all staring up at him. Then he realised they were not looking at him, but at something *above* him.

He rushed out, ran down the dreary corridors, almost fell down the stairs and stumbled through the main entrance. Crunching across the gravel he eventually reached the group of staff in front of the building. He looked up and his worst fear was confirmed. High up on the sloping slate roof sat James. He did not appear to be distressed, and was looking out into the distance.

At first Jenkins wanted to cry out, but then he noticed how still everything was. A pale, golden, evening light lit up the scene. In that serene light the faces of his colleagues seemed strangely dignified, even beautiful. They just stood there, silent and attentive, as if waiting for some important pronouncement.

What *are* we waiting for, thought Jenkins: an almighty splat, or for the majestic power behind the universe to declare itself? All week the enigmatic patient had been the main topic of conversation. Perhaps deep down, hardly acknowledging it and ridiculous as it sounded, they were awaiting a miracle. Something to bring the sad little dramas of their lives to a brilliant and totally unexpected climax. They were waiting for James to float down to the ground: to walk amongst them, touching them and healing their many afflictions. They were hoping against hope for the time of weeping to be finally and irrevocably over.

There was a collective gasp as James stood up precariously on the steeply angled roof.

"What now?" thought Jenkins in anguish. "Are you about to sample flying?"

There was a roar and a splattering of gravel as a car pulled up. Jenkins turned to see Dr Reynolds.

"It's James," he said. "You know, the patient in room 109."

"I know who he is," she snapped.

"My God!"

There were cries of horror. James was no longer on the roof. Jenkins was suddenly immersed in a vast silence that easily absorbed all sound around him. In this eerie stillness even his heart was motionless. Only James moved, approaching slowly, so impossibly slowly. Jenkins thought he saw an expression of surprise, then wry amusement. James embraced the earth, arms fully outstretched and the silence was shattered. An awful sound nobody should ever have to hear hit Jenkins hard. Dr Reynolds was there first. There was nothing she could do. The neck was broken.

That evening Jenkins sat at his laptop in the small, pokey upstairs room he called his office. He was editing his story according to the jottings in his exercise book. He did it in a slow, mechanical way. It was something to do to try to keep away a terrible feeling of loss.

Realising he would be unable to develop the story that evening, he was about to save the file and put the laptop to sleep, when a tremor passed through his body. He waited anxiously for any development. Perhaps it was a delayed reaction to the shock of today?

For a few seconds nothing happened, but then there was only the mad clatter of keys as Jenkins wrote as he had never written in his life before. In a moment of great clarity he had seen the complete resolution to his plot impasse. Mind, fingers and computer were one integrated output stream. Where the creative input was coming from he had no idea. His end of the system was simply to allow words to appear on a display screen. What ecstatic joy to be a part of that flow.

Amy Reynolds sat in front of the television. Her hand shook as she put down her cup of tea. It had been one of the worst days of her life. There had been questions from the police, questions from the director of the institution, and questions from some local reporter, who had been waiting for her as she left to go home.

The worst encounter had been with Tom Dickens, the director. He had a way of making his every utterance sound like a criticism. There would be an inquiry, and no doubt further questions tomorrow.

The thought of tomorrow filled her with dread. She was barely fifty; there should have been plenty of life left in her, but over the years more and more stupid bureaucratic changes had altered her job beyond all recognition. She felt permanently tired from having to meet impossible targets. Tom acted out a macho style of management to hide his incompetence. His idea of leadership was to avoid the word "I" in times of trouble and point fingers.

Images of James rose up in her mind to displace these angry thoughts. Poor James.

The silly excitement on the screen, which up till now she had managed to ignore, was reaching some kind of climax. Curiously, she saw three balls with numbers on them. The numbers were familiar somehow. Why, yes, they were three of the numbers she used every week when filling in her national lottery form.

"Well, that's good," she thought. "It's time I got something back." She had never won anything.

The fourth ball appeared, displaying another one of her numbers. She was now completely alert. She knelt on a rug close to the television screen.

"Oh, my God!" she exclaimed as the fifth number was revealed. Mouth open in shock she waited for the final ball. This is where her luck would abandon her. A lifetime of experience told her the jackpot was beyond her reach. That would take a miracle.

Jenkins, face sweaty, approached the end of the story. With a flourish he keyed in the final sentence: "When gods recover from their self-imposed amnesia, it does not follow that they become immune to the common cold; they continue to experience the usual mishaps, and sometimes they slip up."

THE ENERGY OSBORNE DOCUMENTS

Jack "Energy" Osborne
Born 12 January 1970
Died 14 April 1921

Document #1: Interview on 06 July 2013 with science correspondent Melvyn Pyke

Could you tell us a little about yourself?

My name is Energy Osborne. I'm a successful inventor legally bound not to tell you what I've invented. It was easier to sell my patents to the companies threatened by my ideas than to develop and market them myself, and so the ideas were subsequently buried. It's funny to think I've made so much money from amazing gadgets that never really existed, but this allowed me to buy a large property in Surrey and set up my own private lab. I have the freedom to work on my own project, but the bills keep coming in so my occasional bread-and-butter work is making precision scientific instruments for institutions and university departments round the world. For example, one of my current assignments is making a cheap sensitive gas detector. Incidentally I've realised it could be adapted to make a ripeness sensor for fruit. Imagine your fruit bowl beeping like a smoke detector when your pears approach their half hour of perfection!

Is Energy Osborne your real name?

My real name is Jack, I acquired the nickname "Energy" when I was at university. All my experiments seemed to require a vast amount of energy. My home is fitted with the largest array of solar panels of any domestic property in the UK, and I also have a three-phase electric power supply.

What is your private project?

I'm working on a time machine.

Rather an audacious project for one man working in his garage!

It's hardly a garage, but such things are not impossible. James Lovelock has invented many important detectors working alone in his shed in Devon, and I've met Steve Grand, the writer of "How to build an android in twenty easy steps." He's trying to crack AI, working at home with his wife Ann. My heroes are the little guys: the independent scientists. In earlier centuries there were thousands of us, but nowadays it seems that one needs the cooperation of twenty countries to start a project. However, independent research does still go on.

Okay, so you're trying to build a time machine at home on your own, but it's quite another thing to actually succeed. Does it work?

Yes, it does.

Is there evidence? Have you submitted a paper?

I tried in the early days, but my papers were rejected. I then realised my work was so cutting edge I would have to go it alone. I'm privileged in that for the last twenty years I've been able to devote about half of my time to the project.

I'd like to read you this quote by Richard Horton, editor of *The Lancet*, "We portray peer review to the public as a quasi-sacred process that helps to make science our most objective truth teller. But we know that the system of peer review is biased, unjust, unaccountable, incomplete, easily fixed, often insulting, usually ignorant, occasionally foolish, and frequently wrong."

In other words, Melvyn, the rejections only show that my papers were found unacceptable, not that they are invalid.

So have you travelled in time?

The machine works. I have travelled through time, but – and I admit it's a big "but" – so far only for a few seconds. I've managed to travel back in time three seconds.

Three seconds! Is that all?

I have succeeded in proving that time travel is possible. The small jumps are part of a staged plan of gradually scaling up. But there is always going to be a huge problem in that, although I can transport myself through time, I can't yet transport the equipment, so would never be able to get back. I literally have to live through the time required to get back to the present, which has become my future.

What actually happened?

After activating the machine I suddenly appeared in the room behind myself. I saw myself concentrating on the instruments, press a switch, and disappear. And there I was, feeling discombobulated, but ecstatic!

So you are the pioneer of time travel!

No, I wasn't the first. That honour belongs to Chrono my cat. Of course I would have been devastated if anything had gone wrong, but I had to test the machine. Only Chrono has shared the experience of going back in time; unfortunately he doesn't make for a reliable witness.

Now for the sixty-four thousand dollar question: how does it work?

Would you like a copy of the plans! Suffice it to say it exploits a little-discussed fact: that the so called constants vary slightly. I'm talking about G the Newtonian constant of gravitation, c the speed of light, the fine-structure constant, and so on. I mention these merely as examples of universal constants; I'm not divulging the one actually used in my experiment. It's a controversial subject whether the constants are constant. My discovery is that certain constants can change appreciably, for very short bursts of time, and this can be exploited. If I said any more it would set tongues wagging. That too is a clue.

What kind of clue?

Well in my apparatus the tongue plays a part in "navigating". The tongue is a muscular hydrostat that performs a number of functions, including tasting food. Well it turns out it is also sensitive to certain wave patterns. When I was young my father would test batteries by placing the terminals across his tongue. Although not the same as what I'm talking about, recalling those childhood memories pointed me in the right direction.

What about time paradoxes?

What is most odd is seeing myself. But am I seeing myself? Which is the real me: the one looking or the one I am seeing? I see myself but I know for certain I am not there, because I am "here". There is a blurring of the sense of identity with the body. So far the two Jacks have never gazed at one another. I guess I am somewhat nervous at the thought of meeting my own gaze.

What of the future?

As far as I know I am the first human to have achieved time travel. It seems likely that one day I will be famous. My achievement will be recorded in books. I sometimes wonder whether in the future, when time travel is fully mastered, somebody will be curious to meet the pioneer and come in a time machine to visit me in my lab. Occasionally I get a strange feeling that somebody is in the house even though I know it's empty and the doors locked. I have the impression that things are missing or not quite where I left them. It's rather spooky.

Energy, it's been fascinating talking to you. If you ever need a volunteer, you know where to look!

Thanks for your enthusiasm, but actually that would be unethical, because I couldn't guarantee your safety. In fact, if I disappear it might be because, although I check my calculations many times, something has gone wrong. In that case you should scrutinize the history books carefully for any signs of Energy Osborne. Are there indications of an ancient civilisation being able to perform engineering feats ahead of its time? I promise if I get stranded several millennia back to carve my name in the wall of an ancient temple or monument, except that when I do it the stone will be clean and freshly cut.

Document #2: Text sent to Melvin Pyke from Energy Osborne dated 19 August 2013

Gutted. All my apparatus and computers gone. The entire workroom stripped bare. My online backups hacked. I presume it was government, but which one?

Document #3: Email sent to Melvin Pyke from Energy Osborne dated 20 August 2013

Good morning Melvyn. I'm looking on the bright side: at least I wasn't kidnapped. I'm assuming that if the people who took my stuff wanted to continue its development, they would have taken me too. So perhaps it was an attempt to stop time travel. Some kind of time police perhaps?

Or it was some semi-incompetent who managed to invent time travel after me, but thinks he can get top billing in the history books by eliminating the competition.

Some other good news is that my house was not trashed and Chrono my cat is fine. This was no ordinary burglary. There is no sign of a break-in. Everything to do with my work was clinically removed. Right now I feel like going away. Maybe India?

Document #4: Folder of photographs

The folder contains many photographs showing people and animals sticking their tongues out. It seems that Energy Osborne was especially interested in very long tongues.

Document #5: Statement dated 25 January 2015

My name is John Tissandier. I am one of the admins of a Facebook group called "I AM". The description of the group reads, "The purpose of this group is unknown. Perhaps the purpose of this group is to discover its purpose." However, it would be fair to say that the group discussions are often focused on nonduality. Nonduality, also known as Advaita Vedanta, is one of the core philosophies of Hinduism and teaches the doctrine of not-two, or that in essence there is no separation. A sage who is often quoted in the group is Sri Ramana Maharshi (the reason for mentioning him will become obvious in due course).

I created the group in February 2009. Energy Osborne joined later. He was a lively, active member whose posts were often confrontational. Once he wrote, "I practise the shake 'n' vac. Sometimes I try to shake your ideas; if they are not well grounded they get vacuumed up into the dusty bag of forgotten history." He would write funny stuff like, "If you're enlightened, and you know it, clap one hand!" He could be counter-intuitive, "I dimly recall an eternity of enlightenment. Everything had the same Taste. Every moment was the same. Then one day I became endarkened. Now I'm on an unpredictable roller-coaster ride of infinite ignorance. At last I have desires to enjoy, and there's pizza!"

He mentioned his time machine and there were several discussions about it. Soon after informing us that his machine had been stolen and his project destroyed, he left the group.

Earlier this month I received an astonishing Facebook private message from a woman called Josephine Tutman. She too is a member of the "I AM" group. Currently she lives in South India in a town called Tiruvannamalai, which is the location of the ashram of Ramana Maharshi. Josephine is a frequent visitor to the ashram and as a result learnt of an unusual discovery. In the process of knocking down a hut used by long-term visitors to the ashram, a document was found. The ashram authorities could make no sense of it, but straightaway Josephine realised the importance of the find. She contacted me and sent me a copy of what had remained hidden all these years.

Document #6: Letter from Energy Osborne found at Sri Ramana Ashram

TO WHOM IT MAY CONCERN

The year is 1921. I'm feeling very weak and so this will be brief. I am a time traveller from the future. I was living just south of London and made my last jump in 2013. In the final weeks of my project I was able to increase the power of my machine enormously. I could have gone anytime and anywhere. I could have seen the pyramids being built, or jumped into the unknown future, but instead I chose to meet a sage I consider to be the most remarkable human being who has ever lived. I discovered him via a Facebook group called "I AM". If you are living before 2004 you won't have heard of Facebook. I knew somehow that, of all the possibilities before me, meeting this man was what I wanted to do. And I was not disappointed. When I met the gaze of the Maharshi the peace that had always eluded me came flooding in and was discovered to be my own inalienable nature.

Now there is nothing left for me to do. All desires are extinguished. The only concern left is a fervent hope that Chrono my cat found a new home where he was loved and looked after. During the final weeks in my own time, the sense of being spied on became unbearable and I felt sure events were about to reach a climax. In order to buy a little more time I concocted and spread a story that my machine had been stolen. I ensured that after my final jump the time machine self-destructed. All my notes and data are beyond recovery. I bear the responsibility for what some will consider to be an act of supreme vandalism, but sadly I realised there was no-one I could trust with my invention.

[Editor's note: After the main body of the text there are a few scribbled and disconnected lines. Some are indecipherable.]

The difference between calling life real and calling it a dream is actually very superficial.

Going to see a guru and coming away unenlightened is like buying a doughnut and discovering there's no jam in it.

There are no Bibles and Korans in Heaven. If someone insisted on having a Bible whilst in Heaven it would be the equivalent of choosing porn over a real person.

We come into this world naked without all our fancy theories, and life finds a way to knock them out of us and return us to simplicity.

Shall I tell you where Awareness can go? HERE. That's it! There's nowhere but HERE. And as for time... there isn't any time for Awareness at all, not even NOW. There is only the TIMELESS, which means NO time at all.

Document #7: Postscript

Ashram records show that an English visitor came to stay in 1921. Ramana Maharshi would have been 42 at the time. This was ten years after Ramana's first Western visitor Frank Humphrey and about ten years before the arrival of Paul Brunton, an author who popularised Ramana in the West. The record states that the visitor died a few weeks later from a severe case of dysentery.

THE LAST THING

I am looked after in an environment I can no longer see or hear, and I'm unable to speak to the people there. I'm as innocent as the three monkeys. There is food and a bed, and I eat in bed – I do everything in bed. Sometimes someone holds my hand. My hand still works and I squeeze back, feebly.

They give me a pencil to hold. It's hard writing lying on your back unable to see what you're doing. I guess most of it must come out as illegible gibberish. But sometimes when I write the word "WATER," someone puts a glass to my mouth. It feels as if I'm drinking the word.

When I wake up my first thought is, "Today, I'm not going to die, I will write." I have a few words left in me. In the beginning was the word, and words may be well be the last thing too.

To me the day of death is a blank sheet of paper. I imagine trying to muster every particle of strength I possess, but no word appears on the paper, not a single mark, not even a fullstop.

Outside blank.

Inside blank.

Finally, all peacefully blank.

However, if you approached the bed it would seem as if my hand was forever poised to write...

What words!

What worlds!

OPTIONAL NOTES

6. THE ELUSIVE OBVIOUS
With thanks to Roger Linden.

7. NO MAN
With thanks to Douglas Harding.

8. THE WRONG KIND OF WIND
Published in *Caduceus*, Issue 99.

16. THE BEACH HUTS
Second prize Dawlish Poetry 2017.

22. PARC BENCH rev.1
The unusual spelling refers to the Palo Alto Research Centre in California, where computing as we know it originated, and whose innovations were later copied by Apple and Microsoft.

24. REAL NERDS DON'T NEED COMPUTERS
Fortran is a high-level programming language originally developed in the 1950s.

28. JACQUARD'S DREAM
Joseph Marie Jacquard was a Frenchman, who introduced a special loom in 1801 controlled by punched cards.

30. CRISIS IN EXCELSIS
Published in *International Times*, June 2017.

37. RING OF TREES
This refers to a place on the river path from Totnes to Sharpham, where a friend had a vision of Hermes.

42. SO WHAT'S THE DIFFERENCE?
Jackie Juno is an ex-Grand Bard of Exeter and organiser of Open Mic events in Totnes, where I have performed poems like this one and "ARE YOU LISTENING?" (which is partially improvised).

60. DIVING IN
Trubridge is a world champion freediver from New Zealand.

70. REASONS TO BE CHEERFUL
With thanks to Ian Dury.

87. ONCE I WAS X
The programming languages are arranged not necessarily in the order I learnt them, but in the order in which they appeared (I'm dating Lisp by Common Lisp and not the original version).

92. Fish doing press-ups
The standard theory of evolution can be summarised as: "mutate first, adapt later." The short poem that begins "Fish doing press-ups" expresses an addition to the theory. Here first there is a plastic response to the environment. If it is favourable then that plasticity can determine which random mutations spread.

93. KRYTEN'S LIBRARY
The short poem that begins "To the library" appeared under this title as part of *Between the Covers*, an event celebrating the opening of the new Totnes Library in June 2013.

134. LANDSCAPE WITH THE ALIEN
Based on the painting "Landscape with the Artist" by Cecil Collins.

141. OBSESSION
Appeared in *International Times*, July 2018.

146. PORRIDGE PANCAKES PARADOX
Written on 17 March 2016 in twenty minutes, during one of Julia Robinson's Creative Writing sessions in Totnes.

155. THAT'S NOT WHAT I ORDERED!
The idea for this first came to me during one of Harula Ladd's Friday morning writing workshops in Totnes.

156. THE ALTERNATIVE ELEPHANT STORY
Appeared in *Self Enquiry*, Spring 1996.

159. THE CHALK MOUTH
This was written as a children's story many years ago. It was accepted for publication by the British editor of a magazine called *Cricket*, but later it was rejected by the American editor who thought such an unsympathetic teacher was unsuitable for children!

37786385R00132

Printed in Poland
by Amazon Fulfillment
Poland Sp. z o.o., Wrocław